PEACEMAKER PASS

The girl Morgan found was better than most, even in Denver. They were settled nicely in Morgan's bed and the gunman was just beginning to apply his skills to the girl's breasts. He knew he'd locked the door but it came open anyway, without breaking. The telltale sound was the little squeal in one of the hinges when the door was about half open.

Morgan rolled to the side of the bed opposite the door, landed hard, his pistol in his hand. The girl's scream was cut off.

The light of the lamp flared up and Morgan peeked cautiously over the edge of the bed.

"I'm sorry, Mister Morgan, for having to spoil your fun, but business is business...."

Also in the *Buckskin* Series:

BUCKSKIN #1: RIFLE RIVER
BUCKSKIN #2: GUNSTOCK
BUCKSKIN #3: PISTOLTOWN
BUCKSKIN #4: COLT CREEK
BUCKSKIN #5: GUNSIGHT GAP
BUCKSKIN #6: TRIGGER SPRING
BUCKSKIN #7: CARTRIDGE COAST
BUCKSKIN #8: HANGFIRE HILL
BUCKSKIN #9: CROSSFIRE COUNTRY
BUCKSKIN #10: BOLT-ACTION
BUCKSKIN #11: TRIGGER GUARD
BUCKSKIN #12: RECOIL
BUCKSKIN #13: GUNPOINT
BUCKSKIN #14: LEVER ACTION
BUCKSKIN #15: SCATTERGUN
BUCKSKIN #16: WINCHESTER VALLEY
BUCKSKIN #17: GUNSMOKE GORGE
BUCKSKIN #18: REMINGTON RIDGE
BUCKSKIN #20: PISTOL GRIP
BUCKSKIN #21: PEACEMAKER PASS
BUCKSKIN #22: SILVER CITY CARBINE
BUCKSKIN #23: CALIFORNIA CROSSFIRE
BUCKSKIN #24: COLT CROSSING
BUCKSKIN #25: POWDER CHARGE

BUCKSKIN #21

PEACEMAKER PASS

KIT DALTON

LEISURE BOOKS  NEW YORK CITY

A LEISURE BOOK®

December 2004

Published by

Dorchester Publishing Co., Inc.
200 Madison Avenue
New York, NY 10016

ISBN 0-8439-2619-8

Printed in the United States of America.

BUCKSKIN #21

PEACEMAKER PASS

1

Denver had changed and Lee Morgan wasn't at all certain he liked what he found. There were too damned many people, too many tall buildings and not nearly enough breathing space.

"Another drink, sir?"

Morgan was staring out of the window. It was a huge window, framing a panoramic view of the Rocky Mountains some forty miles distant. The view was breathtaking.

"Mister Morgan, sir. Another drink?" The barkeep spoke a little louder and Morgan's head jerked. Still, it took a moment for the question to soak in.

"Yeah, sure, why the hell not?" Morgan replied, smiling. "Somebody else is picking up the check."

In spite of the pleasant state of his current situation, Morgan was growing both restless and angry. He had been ensconced at the Golden Inn Hotel for nearly ten days. The man he was supposed to have met nearly a week ago had still not shown up. Morgan couldn't get any answers to his questions either, since the telegram he'd received had been unsigned.

The young gunman had wintered alone in a mountain cabin in the Grand Tetons, then moved down to spend the spring in Cheyenne. After a winter of solitude he was ready for some civilization, so he played a lot of poker and, for a change, Lady Luck had bedded with him. He came away with more than three thousand dollars. He also had some fond memories of a few very special nights spent at the Cheyenne Social Club. It was reportedly the most lavish bordello west of the big river. Morgan wouldn't have argued the point.

It was getting on into summer, the 22nd day of July, when the telegram came. It was short and simple.

> Mr. Morgan,
>
> Use the accompanying funds to get yourself to the Golden Inn west of Denver. All will be furnished, ready and waiting for you. I'll join you within two days of your arrival. If I am late, be patient. Enjoy!

Morgan had followed the instructions to the letter. He reasoned that he had nothing to lose. He found exactly what the telegram implied and he had, in fact, enjoyed. Now even that was wearing thin.

He was beginning to think about trying to do some backtracking of the telegraph's origins. It was something with which he was not altogether unfamiliar. He'd learned more than a little about such procedures in several episodes with the Pinkerton Agency. He finally opted to wait one more day before trying to unravel his good fortune.

"Hello. Would you be Mr. Lee Morgan?"

Just the voice could have produced an erection. It was soft, no question of gender, and the words dripped from a pair of very sensuous looking lips.

Morgan finished his drink, eyeing the girl from top to bottom as he did so, and then he said, "If I wasn't, I'd sure as hell lie to you about it."

The girl smiled and licked her sensuous lips. She pushed a vacant barstool aside and slithered between it and Morgan.

"I'm Mariellen Chapel."

Morgan had to fight back the urge to chuckle. He was asking himself how long it had been since he'd been in a chapel.

"You are Lee Morgan, late of Cheyenne?"

"I am, if you're the one who sent me a telegraph cable."

"I didn't, but I'm here on behalf of the man who did. Can you prove you're Lee Morgan?"

"Can you prove you're here for the reason you say?"

"I like you, Mister Morgan," Mariellen Chapel said, stepping back from him now, "so don't do anything that would make me change my mind. Chotauk wouldn't like that even a little bit."

Morgan assumed a quizzical expression and then turned in the direction of Mariellen's pointed finger. By the doorway into the hotel's lobby there stood what Morgan could have very easily mistaken for an adult male polar bear. The Eskimo was six-and-a-half-feet tall and Morgan reckoned about 240 pounds. He looked a little foolish in an ill-fitted, store bought, blue pin stripe. Still, Morgan didn't think it would be healthy to comment on the man's appearance.

"Chotauk?" Morgan asked, pointing and smiling.

"Chotauk," Mariellen confirmed.

"In my room," Morgan said, "I've got the proof." He stood up and made a somewhat dramatic and gentlemanly gesture. "Shall we?"

"I think not," Mariellen said. "You get the proof and bring it here." She glanced around, spotted an empty table in the far corner of the room and added, "Over there will be fine."

Morgan shrugged and said, "Whatever you say, Miss . . . uh, Chapel, wasn't it?"

"It was, Mister Morgan, and it still is." She smiled that sensuous smile and added, "That will make Chotauk very, very happy."

By the time Morgan returned, Mariellen Chapel was very much engaged in devouring a two-inch thick cut of beef and all of the frills. She was dainty and feminine enough about her eating habits but her appetite looked more like it should belong to the big Eskimo.

"Coffee, Mister Morgan?"

Morgan wasn't sure if it was a question or a demand. He nodded, Mariellen poured, refilling her own cup at the same time. She sipped a little of it and then sat back. "Your proof, please."

He handed her a sheaf of papers and she studied each with the intensity of a spider examining the latest victim trapped in its web. Morgan suddenly felt like the fly.

After nearly a quarter of an hour, with Morgan getting a little more disgusted with the passing of each minute, Mariellen removed two of the sheets and handed Morgan the balance.

A wave of her arm brought Chotauk to the

table in about five strides. She handed him the papers and he eyed Morgan, then nodded.

"He may have a little trouble checking those out," Morgan said, "they go back aways."

"You'd best hope he doesn't, Mister Morgan. If he finds any discrepancies, he'll kill you."

"You'd order him to do that?"

Mariellen smiled. "I wouldn't have to," she said and then leaned forward and added, "and once he started, I couldn't stop him."

Morgan considered the girl. Really she was more a girl-woman. There was much about her that appeared young and innocent, but there was an equal part of a mature, shrewd and very hard lady.

"When do I meet the bossman," Morgan finally asked, offhandedly. "Or are you the boss lady?"

"If you are who you claim to be, you'll be on my payroll, Mister Morgan. If you're as good as my friend tells me you are, you may even live to spend your wages."

"And what if I don't want the job?"

"One step at a time, Mister Morgan, one step at a time."

Mariellen ordered some after dinner wine and this time she didn't ask if he wanted any, she just poured. A moment later, she broke out a shiny, hand engraved silver case. Somewhere out of sight there was a catch release and when she pushed it, the lid popped open. "A cigareet," she asked.

The cigareet, as Mariellen called it, wasn't half bad. Morgan made a mental note that he'd have to buy some of these store bought smokes. This one was his first. He was just finishing his second glass of wine, and feeling an inside warmth which was a dangerous mingling of the wine and the proximity of Mariellen Chapel, when her face broke into a very wide smile.

"I'm glad you are Morgan," she said, a little quiver of lightness in her tone, "very glad."

Morgan frowned and Mariellen pointed. Morgan saw Chotauk was back and he was also smiling, a toothless smile.

"I checked out."

She nodded.

"Then it's my turn to ask the questions."

"Not yet, Mister Morgan, not quite yet." She got to her feet and Morgan started to rise but she held out her hand. "Stay put, finish the wine, enjoy yourself. This is your last evening in Denver and it's going to have to serve you for quite a spell. Goodnight, Mister Morgan."

Morgan said nothing. He could only wonder about Miss Mariellen Chapel. What he wondered was not all printable, but then it was the only safe way to do anything where Mariellen Chapel was concerned. Morgan watched Mariellen go up the stairs. Chotauk was only a few feet behind.

Morgan found a Keno game and dropped two hundred dollars on it. He walked around two or three of Denver's blocks and then returned to the hotel. He asked a few of the bellhops and two or three of the people behind the desk about Mariellen. They would say nothing, although he was certain that most of them were lying. He was certain she was in the hotel, and he was damned certain he wanted to know her better. At that moment, his reasoning had little else to do but remember the rise and fall of Mariellen's blouse.

The girl he found was better than most, even in Denver. She was young, well proportioned and inexpensive. Morgan rarely needed the services of a professional but it had been a long dry spell and the whisky, beer, wine and visions of Mariellen caught up with him.

They were settled nicely in Morgan's bed and the gunman was just beginning to apply his skills to the girl's breasts. He knew he'd locked the door but it came open anyway, without breaking. The tell-tale sound was the little squeal in one of the hinges when the door was about half open.

Morgan rolled to the side of the bed opposite the door, landed hard, his pistol in his hand. The girl's scream was cut off.

The light of the lamp flared up and Morgan peeked cautiously over the edge of the bed.

"I'm sorry, Mister Morgan, for having to spoil your fun, but business is business and you represent a considerable investment."

"Sonuvabitch," Morgan said, softly but aloud. He got to his knees. In the hallway behind Mariellen Chapel, he could see the struggling girl. She appeared the size of a rabbit in the clutches of Chotauk. "Lady, you're pushing me a helluva lot harder than any man would get away with, but I've got a limit even on that."

Mariellen ignored Morgan and continued tearing at the bedding. She finally found one of the girl's red garters. She eyed it and then Morgan, noticing for the first time his rather unmanly position. She smiled and tossed his longjohns and pants.

"Did your lady friend mention anything about a drink?"

Morgan got his pants on and walked around the end of the bed. "Yeah, something special after we finished." He was surprised that Mariellen knew, surprised and mad all at once.

"It would have been special indeed," she said.

He frowned.

The garter was decorated with a tiny locket. Inside there was a pinch of white powder.

"I'd guess powdered quinela. That's enough to kill a horse."

"Are you telling me that, uh, young lady, was a set up?"

"I'm not telling you anything, Mister Morgan, except what I told you earlier. My suggestion is that you get back in that bed and try to get some sleep. You're going to need it."

Morgan was awake for nearly two more hours but only because he was trying to make some kind of sense out of what he knew at that moment. It was damned little and it made no sense at all. He finally drifted off and slept fitfully until the first rays of the new day's sun poked through the window.

Morgan washed, shaved, dressed and made two vows to himself. He'd begin the day with what could be the last really good meal he'd be getting for awhile and before the sun was gone again, he'd have some answers. Either that, or he'd be gone.

2

"Good morning, Mister Morgan." Mariellen Chapel spoke as she glanced up at the big wall clock in the hotel's dining room. There was a dirty plate in front of her and a half empty coffee cup. "Will you have breakfast?" she asked him, grinning, "or lunch?"

"You sure as hell look good for a lady who couldn't have gotten that much sleep."

"I don't require much," she said.

"Sleep?"

Mariellen smiled. "Yeah, sleep. Isn't that what we were talking about?"

By the time Morgan got his hat off and seated himself, the waiter had arrived with a pot of fresh coffee.

"Breakfast, sir?"

"He'll have the same as I had," Mariellen said. "A cut of your best beefsteak, two eggs on the sunny side and some black bread."

The waiter poured the coffee, nodded and was gone before Morgan could protest.

Mariellen seemed to sense that he was going to

do just that so she made her next revelation. "The young lady you so graciously took into your room last night hung herself this morning. Got up on the roof," Mariellen said, pointing straight up, "lashed a rope around an air vent, tightened the noose around her neck and jumped."

"Lady," Morgan said, his tone harsh now, "I'd better get an awful lot of the right answers in a very damned short time."

"Or what, Mister Morgan?"

"Or you can send off another telegraph cable and see what the bait brings this time."

Mariellen smiled and glanced toward the door. Morgan understood her meaning and took her by the wrist, hard. "And if the polar bear tries to stop me, ma'am, I'll kill him."

Chotauk moved almost at the same instant Morgan took a grip on Mariellen's wrist but he stopped when Mariellen raised her other hand. "I believe you'd try, Mister Morgan, I really do."

"You can count on it. Now, how about some answers?" Morgan detected the first doubtful look he'd seen in the girl's face.

Nonetheless, she smiled and recouped quickly. "One more little extension, Mister Morgan, just bear with me for a little longer." She glanced toward the kitchen. "Just until you've finished your breakfast."

"You stay put in the meantime, right there where I can keep an eye on you, Miss Chapel, and you've got yourself a deal."

"Agreed," she replied, tentatively.

Morgan ate his breakfast in silence. Mariellen smoked two of the cigareets, and drank two cups of coffee.

Morgan accepted another of Mariellen's smokes to go with his last cup of coffee. He noted that she had begun to fidget and glance, frequently, toward the door.

"You expecting company?" he finally asked.

She was about to answer when her face took on the sudden glow of a big smile of relief. Morgan jerked his head around and saw Chotauk pointing toward the table. Standing next to him was a tall, slender, distinguished looking gentleman, armed, as far as Morgan could see, with an official looking attache case.

Mariellen got to her feet and half ran to meet the man. She threw her arms around his neck and gave him a kiss on the cheek. Morgan wasn't surprised when Mariellen introduced him.

"Morgan, this is my uncle, Harrison Chapel. He hails all the way from Alexandria, Virginia."

Morgan got to his feet and took the man's hand. It was soft, almost feminine to the touch. This man was not a westerner, not a laborer, of those things only, Morgan was certain.

"Please," Harrison Chapel said, "sit down and finish your breakfast."

"I'm finished," Morgan said, "at least with breakfast."

"I owe you an apology, sir. I am usually more punctual."

"I hope so," Morgan replied, reclaiming his chair. The girl moved over one chair and Harrison Chapel took her old spot. He immediately unlocked and opened the attache case, removed a document and handed it to Morgan.

Agent Agreement

The following agreement is hereby entered into between the Colt Firearms Mfg. Co. and Lee Morgan. This agreement will not be bound by date or time and will commence upon signing by Lee Morgan. It will remain in force and in effect until a termination of the duties requested, or the permanent disability or death of Lee Morgan, or a decision by two-thirds of the then acting Board of Directors of the Colt Firearms Mfg. Co.

The Company agrees to a recompense for Lee Morgan as follows: All expenses incurred in the line of his duties, plus $25,000 severance bonus.

Morgan looked up, eyed both Harrison Chapel and Chapel's niece and looked down again at the paper. There was room on the bottom for three signatures. His own, he reckoned, an agent for the Colt Company, and likely a witness.

"I was told last night that if I accepted the job I'd be working for you, Miss Chapel."

"You will, at a regular wage. That's the only way you'll be able to move around and have half a chance to do the job for my uncle."

"You work for Colt?"

"I'm a special representative in the territory."

"What territory?" Morgan asked.

The Chapels, for the first time, looked at one another with expressions of doubt. Harrison Chapel finally looked back at Morgan, sighed heavily and said, "Alaska, Mister Morgan. My company wants you to go to Alaska. We've got big troubles up there and they will only get worse unless we can find a man good enough to stand up to the country and the evil in it."

"That's real damned pretty talk," Morgan said, shoving his chair back from the table. His eyes shifted from Harrison Chapel to Mariellen and he gestured with his head, adding, "And you've got some real pretty bait, too." He stood up. "The only thing you don't have is guts enough to come straight out and ask a man to do a job." Morgan tossed some money on the table and turned to walk away. He paused, turned back and added, "And the other thing you don't have is Lee Morgan."

Chotauk was already moving in Morgan's direction but Morgan didn't stop. Behind him, Mariellen Chapel held up her hand, Chotauk stopped and stepped aside.

Morgan hadn't broken his stride and as he drew parallel with the big Eskimo he spoke once again, loudly enough to make certain he was heard. "That was a damned smart thing to do, Miss Chapel." He looked squarely into Chotauk's eyes as he passed by.

Morgan wasted no time in packing his gear and making ready to ride out of Denver. He wasn't certain just where he'd go but he'd had enough of the easy life to last him awhile. It made a man soft and careless and if the man was Lee Morgan, that was dangerous. He'd made a lot of enemies of his own and those who didn't know him personally knew him by reputation, one not altogether of his own making. He was, after all, the son of no less a gunman than Buckskin Frank Leslie. One of the best or the worst of a breed, depending on which end of his gun you had to face.

Morgan couldn't help but think of Mariellen Chapel as he packed. He wouldn't be any kind of a man at all if he could ignore what he was certain was under the silk and satin. Between her and twenty-five thousand dollars, he could have quite a bulge in his buckskin britches. He could also end up in the clutches of that polar bear in the pin stripe suit or pushing up flowers in a six-by-six hole in Alaska.

The knock at the door was hard enough to tell Morgan that whoever was doing it wasn't trying to keep it a secret. Still, he was cautious. "Yeah, who is it?"

"Delivery, sir."

Morgan frowned and thought that the Chapels were making a last ditch effort. "Return it," he said.

Morgan heard the delivery boy or bellhop or whoever the hell was outside, walk away. He was also certain he'd heard them put the package by the door. He opened it and his suspicion was confirmed. The package was about three feet by two feet and some ten inches deep. Morgan looked both ways but saw no one. He moved the package carefully with the toe of his boot. It was heavy.

"Damn," Morgan muttered.

He picked it up and took it inside his room. He put it on the bed and then stared at it. His curiousity had led the young gunman into more adventures than he cared to recall and he figured it would, one day, be his downfall. "A parting gesture of good will from the Chapels," he said aloud, grinning. "Bullshit! Another temptation." He couldn't help but wonder if the package might contain twenty-five thousand dollars. He decided to stop wondering.

The holsters were matched as beautifully as were the weapons reposing in them. The case's lining was satin and velvet, a soft purple in color. The two weapons were nickel plated, ivory gripped Colt .45 Peacemakers. The grips displayed his initials on each and the outside barrels were also engraved.

Presented to Lee Morgan for Services Rendered to the Colt Firearms Mfg. Co. in Alaska, U.S. Territory

Morgan hefted the weapons and quickly realized their quality. The balance was perfect, the grips seemed almost as if they had been personally molded to his hand. He was not a two gun man but here were weapons that any man would be proud to own, to wear or simply to display.

He felt the warmth on his cheeks, the warmth of his anger. Most of it was anger that he was directing at himself. He was a loner, he always had been. He was set in his ways. He liked to be approached openly. Unsigned telegraph cables, sudden confrontations with beautiful women, threats from their bodyguards, young girls who tried to poison him and then tossed themselves off of rooftops, and business representatives who were a week late with appointments did not make up his idea of good business conduct. Still, he was flattered by the offer from so prestigious a firm as Colt. Too, he couldn't deny what had happened, someone had tried to kill him. He'd never been to Alaska, another reason to slow his judgment down. Then, of course, there was Mariellen Chapel.

"Damn," Morgan mumbled.

3

During the next several weeks, Morgan had plenty of time to digest the information he acquired from Harrison Chapel. He learned that Chapel had been in the employ of the Colt Company for more than a decade. During that time he had served the company in nearly every capacity, from demonstrating new guns and new designs, to negotiating with foreign governments in an effort to secure contracts. Never, during all of that time, had Chapel failed to deliver on his assignment. Never, that is, until two years ago.

Chapel was to carry the Colt name to the last frontier, Alaska. The gold and silver strikes in the raw, hard territory were only just beginning and every form of life, high and low, four legged and two, was scrambling to get in on the boom.

The Colt Company, of course, was by no means the only weapons maker anxious to cut a sizeable share of profit out of the frozen tundra but, at first, it was the only one willing to do it above board. The decision had taken four lives to date.

At the outset of the effort, Chapel was

confident he could quickly secure a base of business for the Colt Company. He had the expertise, and something else which his competition did not have . . . a resident representative.

Mariellen Chapel's parents had been killed on the 31st day of May, 1889. They were two of a reported two-thousand who died on that fateful day in the sleepy hamlet of Johnstown, Pennsylvania. Flood waters took their lives and their remains. As it happened, 19-year-old Mariellen was visiting her aunt and uncle at the time.

Mariellen had had a promising career in nursing and medicine. There had even been talk of her attempting to enter medical school to become a doctor. None of it mattered to her after the disaster, and one day she was simply gone. Three years later, Harrison Chapel got the first word of her whereabouts. She was in Alaska and was known far and wide as the Queen of the Klondike.

When the time came for Harrison Chapel to open the market for the Colt Company, he sent his best man to Mariellen. His best man ended up dead. So did the three men who followed. Mariellen's own troubles increased as well when the word began to circulate that she had a contact with the Colt Company.

Harrison Chapel made the trip north, personally did some investigating of his own into the problem, and then decided upon a course of action.

Chapel's plan was simple enough. First he had to restore the credibility enjoyed by his niece. Mariellen had built her reputation as Queen of the Klondike, in part, on greed. Chapel could only put his own man in place if he was able to convince the locals that Mariellen had also turned on him. He managed that with a highly visible and carefully orchestrated confrontation. Mariellen emerged the apparent victor and enjoyed an even more powerful position than before.

Now, almost nothing moved between Skagway and Dawson without first passing through Mariellen Chapel's fingers. The word was quickly spread that newcomers would be better advised to tackle the infamous Chilkoot Pass in winter than defy the Queen of the Klondike.

Harrison Chapel then delivered his *coup de grâce* by aligning himself with no less a figure than Mariellen's predecessor to the territory. She was known as Skagway Annie. In fact, she was Annabelle Thompson, and one of the most colorful characters ever to appear in the territory.

While her background was obscure, her appearance in Skagway had preceded even some of the hardiest men. She smoke cigars, chewed a tobacco named M.D. which the locals dubbed "Moose Dung" and turned the air blue with her expletives.

Morgan knew that much about the operation he was getting into by the time he arrived in San Francisco, the first week in September. Once there, he learned that the next available passage to Juneau was three weeks away. He spent that three weeks living in luxury in a prepaid suite at the Mark Hopkins Hotel. On his last day in San Francisco, he used the telephone instrument to order up room service. After a supper of steak and champagne, he poured himself a real drink, then walked over to the window to look out over the town. He held the glass up to the window and made a quiet toast to the city.

"A few weeks from now I'll be ass-deep in snow, so if I'm indulging myself a little now, I got it comin' to me."

On September 25, Lee Morgan, gunman and special representative for the Colt Company, boarded the steam packet *Arctic Mist.* He was told by the purser that it would be a trip of fifteen days.

The *Arctic Mist* was crowded with men who were going to Alaska to hunt gold.

"They say in Nome you can scoop it up right on the beaches."

"Nuggets big as robins' eggs, they say."

"Heard of a fella from Seattle went up there, spent just two months, come back with enough money to live in luxury the rest of his life."

"I got me a system, guaranteed to find gold. I'll be willin' to sell it to anyone wants it for a hunnert dollars. A hunnert dollars'll get you ten thousand, I guarantee it."

He was ten days out when he saw the envelope. It had been slipped under his door from the passageway. Morgan had been lying on his bunk with his hands folded behind his head, wondering what lay ahead, so he didn't see it right away. He just happened to look over and there was the envelope.

The confusion as to how the envelope got into his room was nothing compared to the confusion as to why it was pushed under his door. When he picked it up it was totally empty. It did have a rather unique mark . . . not a postmark, but a type of official seal. He opened the door and looked out into the passageway, but saw no one. There was no one on deck either. He walked over to the rail and looked out over the deep blue sea toward the distant horizon where the merger was so indistinct that there was no line of demarcation between sky and sea. He felt as if he were suspended in a great, blue bowl, and he turned away from the rail wishing he had a horse under him and a mountain in front.

At Juneau he caught a mail packet up to Skagway. His arrival in Skagway was hardly spectacular. It was already dark, though it was the middle of the afternoon. He didn't know his way around, and nobody had bothered to meet him. He got less than a pleasant reception from the few men he queried about the location of Mariellen's place. He knew it only by name, "The Queen's Throne."

He learned right off that anyone asking its whereabouts was quickly recognized as a newcomer, therefore an outsider, therefore competition, and therefore, unwelcome as hell.

Mariellen was in her office. The man who escorted Morgan from the front door did so without a word, walking slightly behind him. Morgan was, briefly at least, sandwiched between the sullen doorman and an old friend. Or perhaps acquaintance would be a better word. Chotauk looked down on Morgan from lofty heights, nodded at the doorman and then opened the door.

"Come in, Morgan," a woman's voice called from within the room. Morgan eyed the Eskimo, then stepped around him to get inside. He saw Mariellen hunched over a ledger book.

"You knew it was me?"

"I knew you were in Skagway when the boat docked."

"Yeah, well, thanks for the warm welcome," Morgan said, though he knew his sarcasm was lost on her. She neither stopped working, nor looked up. Instead she said, "Fix yourself something to drink. I'll be a few minutes yet, then we'll talk."

Mariellen's few minutes turned into half-an-hour. Morgan went through three drinks and one of her cigareets. Finally she slammed the book shut, shoved it aside, sat back in her chair, smiled and said, "You read my uncle's report?"

Morgan nodded.

"Questions?"

"Just one for now. Who the hell are you fighting?"

"That's why you're here Morgan, to find out."

"Your uncle seems to think it's his competition. Remington or Winchester or that English outfit, uh, what's their names?"

"Huntington Armory."

"Yeah." Morgan shifted in his chair. "I think he's wrong."

In fact, Morgan hadn't formed any opinions at all yet but he wanted to test the waters. He got a surprise.

"So do I. I think he's dead wrong."

Morgan frowned.

"None of those people believe they can dominate the sales in Alaska any more than they could back in the States."

"Colt did a pretty good job of it for quite awhile."

"No they didn't, and you know it, Morgan. They got more publicity for a while and they sold more of one or two models than some of the others, but they never came close to all of it."

"Yeah, you're right," Morgan said, getting up and pouring himself another drink. "Who then, if not the competition?"

"Somebody who wants complete control of Alaska and if they control enough weapons and men they can get what they want."

"Somebody like the Queen of the Klondike?"

"Somebody who really is what I'm supposed to be."

"And how do I know you aren't what you seem to be?"

"You don't Morgan," Mariellen said, getting to her feet. She walked around the desk.

Morgan eyed her. She had on a full, heavy cotton skirt, plaid wool shirt and vest. It didn't flatter her but his memory was too vivid to be blotted out by cold weather wear.

"You don't know much of anything about anything right now and worse, you don't know this country or the people in it. We're a different breed, Morgan. You have to be, or the Klondike and the Yukon will swallow you whole."

"I heard the same tale about Texas, New Mexico, Arizona and the Oklahoma badlands."

"That's the difference," Mariellen said, smiling, "down there you hear tales. Up here, you see the real thing."

Morgan considered her. He took off his hat, scratched his head, looked down and then up again, up into Mariellen's eyes.

"Your uncle may be right, maybe he's wrong, but at least he's got an opinion. What have you got?"

"A long hard day tomorrow, Morgan, so I'll say goodnight."

"I hope you don't end up making me wish I was back in San Francisco."

"Chotauk will show you to your room."

Morgan smiled. "He going to tuck me in, too?"

Mariellen walked to the door, opened it, turned

around and said, "Only if you need tucking in, Morgan."

As the young gunman passed Mariellen, she gently touched his arm. He stopped. Maybe, he thought, she will soften up just a little.

"Beginning tomorrow, unless we're strictly in private, you address me as Miss Mariellen. Is that understood?"

Morgan smirked, looked at his boots and shook his head. "You bet it is," he said. Then he looked into her face again and added, "G'night, Miss Mariellen."

The room was at the front of the building, a corner room with a good view of the main street of Skagway. It was a town which rarely slept, and Morgan sat in the dark for some time just watching the men below coming and going. He had started to doze off when he heard the click of the doorknob. His pistol was at the ready when the door slowly opened.

He could see the trim figure of a woman. He waited until she had closed the door before he rose and turned up the lamp. She was more girl than woman. She smiled and handed him a note.

I owe you this from Denver.
Enjoy her and sleep well!
The Boss Lady

"You come with me," Morgan said, his face warm with a building anger. The girl had to double time it to keep up with him as he headed down the long hallway. Mariellen Chapel's private quarters were at the far end of the building. When he turned the corner, it dawned on him that she would be well protected. Indeed, there was a youngster in front of her door. He realized that even Chotauk had to sleep sometime.

The youth looked up but when he saw the girl he just smiled. "Evenin', Clara," he said, grinning.

The grin faded when Morgan stopped directly in front of him.

"Wake up Miss Mariellen," Morgan said. He properly judged the boy and already had the barrel of his gun jammed into the boy's belly. "No arguments."

The kid reached behind himself and pounded on the door. Instantly, the next door down the corridor opened and Chotauk stepped through it. Almost at the same time, Mariellen opened her door. Morgan shoved the girl past her, stepped into the room behind the girl, and then slammed the door closed with the heel of his boot.

"We need a few things understood, boss lady," Morgan said. "I pick my own bed partners or they pick me, and then it's by mutual consent. Right now, you don't owe me a thing."

"I meant no offense."

The door opened and Morgan's Colt flew into his hand as he spun around. Chotauk stood in the doorway. Morgan eyed Mariellen.

"It's alright," she said.

The Eskimo eyed Morgan, eyed the pistol, grinned and backed out, closing the door as he did.

"No," Morgan said, holstering the gun, "it isn't alright. A helluva lot of things are not alright. I'll work for you and I'll do the job. If I don't, you don't owe me anything but you never *own* me, lady. Let's get that straight right now."

"Is that what you think I want to do, Morgan, own you?"

"Yeah, as a matter of fact, that's exactly what I think you want to do. Just like you own Chotauk." Morgan walked over to her. "I'm not Chotauk and I'm not one of your hired gunnies."

"Then why did you take the job?"

"That's my business. You don't like me being the way I am, I'll be on the next boat south, no obligations on either side."

Mariellen Chapel smiled at the girl and then nodded her head in the direction of the door. The girl smiled and quickly took her leave. "My uncle hired you, not me, but it has to look right."

"I'll make it look like whatever is necessary," Morgan said. "I just don't want you to forget that it's just acting, not the real thing."

"I don't know you well enough to judge the real thing, do I?"

Morgan slipped one arm around Mariellen's shoulders and the other around her waist. He pulled her to him and kissed her, hard and full and long. He felt the sensations and they quelled his anger. She did not struggle or protest.

He stepped back. "Start with that," Morgan said. He moved quickly to the door and then turned around, "I've got a busy day ahead," he said, grinning as he echoed her words, "so I'll say goodnight, Miss Mariellen."

4

It seemed to Morgan that all he had done lately was receive odd messages from anonymous authors. One had been slipped under his door during the night. This one had not been accompanied by a girl.

> I'd take it kindly if you'd
> breakfast with me. I'll find
> you. Thompson's Cove. 7:30.

Skagway didn't look much different to Morgan than any other boom town he'd seen. Indeed, the Klondike could have been almost anywhere in Colorado. He paused outside Thompson's Cove and looked north. There, he thought, is the difference. North of Skagway was the Yukon territory. Across a bit of British Columbia and over the Chilkoot Pass, north and east to Whitehorse and back northwest along the rugged trail to Dawson.

Thompson's Cove was different than anything Morgan had ever seen. It was, he thought, a

Herman Melville narrative carved from spruce, pine and cedar. It would have been right at home in Boston, Morgan imagined, or in the legendary seafaring town of New Bedford.

"You've a table waitin' for you, Mister Morgan."

Morgan eyed the speaker. He was bearded and he looked, for all the world, like he'd just stepped off the deck of a four-master.

Morgan was still looking around. This was not the saloon of a frontier. No batwing doors, no gunmen lining the bar, no card sharps dealing house games at the tables.

"At whose invitation?" Morgan finally asked.

"Miss Annie Thompson," the bearded man replied, and then grinned and said, "Miss Skagway Annie to you."

The man gestured toward the table and Morgan moved to it. The table was private, reposing beneath an archway along the east wall. There were several of them. The place settings were already there. The silver trappings and linen cloth were all mongrammed.

"Thanks," Morgan said, removing his hat and ducking a little in order to slide into the seat.

The man left, replaced by an attractive young girl attired in a peasant blouse and pinafore. Morgan's eyes followed the gentle undulations of her breasts as she poured his coffee and made ready the dishware for the serving of the food. She caught him looking once and smiled. He smiled back.

"Lee Morgan. You're younger than I thought. Younger than I heard, but then Chappy is probably not the best judge of men anyway. Guns maybe, but not men."

Morgan looked up.

Annie Thompson was, by Morgan's reckoning, on the sunset side of forty. Her face was a giveaway. There were none of the luxuries in Skagway which kept a woman looking younger than her years. Conversely, Skagway Annie had the body of a woman ten years her junior. Nothing back home to keep a woman fit and trim, Morgan thought. He also thought that her bust measurement would probably be a match for her age. He started to get up.

"Don't bother," she said. "You go and get gentlemanly on me and I'll come to expect if from the rest of the flotsam that drift in here. That'll just upset me, 'cause I won't get it." Annie sat down.

Breakfast arrived at once and while Annie ate, much like Mariellen Chapel, Morgan rather picked at his food. He caught more than one look of disdain. A man who couldn't devour half a polar bear and a quart of bad whiskey for breakfast, so Morgan had been told, would never survive in the Klondike.

"I hate to be pushy," Morgan finally said, "but just why am I here?"

"Because I invited you," came the reply, "and turnin' down an invite from Skagway Annie is mighty bad for a fella's well bein'. Matter o' fact, it's proved plumb fatal in a case or two."

"So you invited me just to see if I'd come and now that I have you can lay claim to having saved my life." Morgan leaned back. "That makes me obligated, doesn't it?"

Morgan's tongue-in-cheek assessment of Annie's motives took her aback for a moment and then she burst out laughing.

"By God Morgan, I like you, I really do like

you. I'll be honest, when Chappy told me about you, I didn't think I would. I mean, I was *sure* I wouldn't. Another driftin' gunhand come to God's country to right ever'body's wrongs."

Morgan finished his coffee. "What do you want, Miss Thompson?" Morgan set his cup down and leaned forward.

"I want you to come to work for me."

"Not interested, I've got a job."

"No you haven't. You're on a payroll over to that high classed whore's place. I'm offerin' you a job."

"I'm not interested."

Now it was Skagway Annie who leaned forward. They were nose to nose across the table. "Then get interested, Mister Morgan, or get out of the Klondike."

"No other alternatives?"

"Just one. You can get interested, or get dead."

"Why do you want me working for you?"

"I don't," Annie said, "Chappy does."

Morgan had assumed, correctly, that the "Chappy" to whom Annie was making reference was, in fact, Harrison Chapel. He assumed also that the meeting was a part of Chapel's plan to further promote the alleged feud between himself and his niece. Morgan sensed that the feud between Skagway Annie and The Queen of the Klondike, Mariellen Chapel, didn't need any help.

Morgan got to his feet. "Like I said before, I'm not interested."

Annie got to her feet, carefully considering the young, handsome gunman. "Tch, tch," she muttered, "too bad. The whore probably pays better, but I offer benefits she can't begin to match."

"No reason we can't be friends," Morgan said, putting on his hat.

"Yeah there is. I don't dally much with dead men."

Annie turned on her heel and walked away. Morgan watched her go back upstairs. He eyed the man who'd met him at the door and then realized two other men had drifted in while he and Annie were breakfasting. These men didn't look like they belonged in a place like Thompson's Cove. No, Morgan thought, they looked more the cut of men he was used to seeing. Both wore hip pistols, tied down rigs with weather worn holsters. They were some fifteen feet apart, standing at the bar. Morgan headed for the door.

"Hey you."

Morgan kept walking.

"Hey! I'm talkin' to you mister, you with the fancy hatband."

Morgan had spotted two bannister poles at the head of the stairway when he came in. Atop each was a small, hand carved parrot. By his estimate he would be about sixty to seventy feet away from them when he reached the door. They were also well above him and would require careful placement of shots if he was to do what he was thinking about.

"Unfriendly sonofabitch, ain't he?" The observation came from the second man.

Morgan reached the door, his back to both men and the stairway. He'd loaded the sixth chamber on the Bisley Colt before he kept his appointment. Now, he was ready. He stopped, bent his knees ever so slightly, drew in a blur, whirled and fired. Left side, right side, gun returned to holster, all in a single, quicker than the eye movement. The parrots were gone. Morgan straightened.

"Either of you gents want to see it again?"

The men's faces gave Morgan his answer.

Annie, with Harrison Chapel at her side, now stood at the head of the stairway.

Morgan glanced up. "You saved one life this morning," he said, looking straight at Annie, "I just saved two. Now you owe me."

He looked back at the two gunmen. One of them, the one who'd made the demeaming comment, was toying with his gun butt.

"Don't even think about it," Morgan said.

"You threatenin' me, mister?"

Morgan's face broke into a broad grin. He shook his head, glanced up again and then back to the man. "Not at all. Just a bit of friendly advice from an unfriendly sonofabitch!" He turned and walked out.

Upstairs, Skagway Annie Thompson had a frown on her face. Though neither of them had seen what had happened, both she and Harrison Chapel had seen the results. Chapel was smiling. "I was right, by God! He's our man, that's sure."

Annie looked up at him, still frowning. She looked at the evidence of Morgan's work and then at her two men. She was still frowning and she didn't comment on Chapel's observation.

Morgan spent most of the rest of the morning just sizing up Skagway and its male population. The only men he had seen so far who looked like possible trouble were the two at Thompson's Cove. He finally went back to Mariellen's place some three hours later.

"Where the hell have you been?"

"Keeping an appointment," Morgan replied, calmly. "I had breakfast with Skagway Annie."

Mariellen glanced around, there was no one close. She smiled. Her uncle had baited the trap.

"You have the regular breakfast?" Mariellen asked, grinning and looking into Morgan's face, "or the house special?"

"The regular I'd guess, but with a last meal option."

Mariellen looked puzzled for a moment and then said, "Cole and Pascal? Gun hands? One older gent an' a smirky lookin' kid?" When Morgan nodded she said, "They're both pretty good."

"I wouldn't know. All I did was kill a couple of wooden parrots."

Mariellen considered him for a moment, then laughed and shook her head. "Well, no matter. You're back and you're breathin'. Now, I've got a job for you. I've got a shipment of supplies comin' up from San Francisco. They'll be unloaded at Juneau on Friday. I want you and Chotauk to take the mail packet down, and be there waitin'."

"I don't need a nursemaid."

"You and Chotauk," Mariellen repeated, her tone firm. "Friday at Juneau. I want you to keep a close eye on the shipment coming back. Half of it is guns . . . rifles, mostly."

Morgan would rather have gone alone, but if he had to deal with the big Eskimo, better that he be on the boat with him.

"I'll watch it," he promised.

* * *

The trip down was about as exciting as a funeral. Chotauk never said a word. He just stood on the deck watching the wake roll out from the bow. He looked around at Morgan, disapprovingly, only once. That was the time Morgan started humming, "Sweet Betsy from Pike."

Juneau was the San Francisco, or, if you preferred, the New York of the territories. Almost nothing could reach the citizens deep in the Klondike or the Yukon which did not first pass through Juneau. It wasn't nearly as cold as Skagway, even though the distance between them was not that great. The difference in temperature came from the fact that Juneau, like Seattle, was warmed by the Japanese current. It was wild and wooly, tough and beautiful, dangerous and damned expensive.

When they got off the boat in Juneau, it was late Thursday night. Chotauk led the way to a big hotel with the rather unimaginative name of Midnight Sun. It was the only tri-story building in Juneau and one of only half a dozen which was built partially of brick. Morgan got his first surprise.

"You stay," Chotauk said. "I go back to boat."

"What the hell's the matter with you staying too?"

Chotauk frowned at Morgan's incompetence. "No allow Eskimo," he said simply. He turned and walked back toward the dock. Morgan looked around, catching a few expressions of disapproval for even being seen in company with an Eskimo.

"You don't really want to stay in this hotel, do you, mister?" a kid asked. He was about ten.

The kid was a hustler. Morgan eyed him and remembered back to his youth and his work as a stable boy. He, too, was a hustler, working on the streets of Grover, Idaho.

"I'd planned on it, yes."

"If you do, you'd better hire someone to keep a watch on your room. Else when you go out for dinner someone'll come along and take your tack."

"I see," Morgan said, smiling at the boy. "And do you happen to have any idea of who I might get to take care of that little job for me?"

"Me," the kid said. "I'll do it."

"I just thought you might. And how much is this going to cost me?"

"Ten bucks."

"Ten dollars? Isn't that a little high?"

"This here is Alaska, mister, an' ten dollars is a lot cheaper'n the other way."

"What other way?"

"You leave your stuff in your room and it gets stole. Then you'll wind up freezin' to death."

"I only have two choices, is that what you're tellin' me? Pay you ten dollars to watch my room and gear, or not pay you and have it stolen."

"There is another way."

Morgan frowned. "That right? And how's that?"

"You come stay at my house with me an' my sis an' you pay twenty dollars and your stuff is safe."

"What do they call you, son?"

"Name's Allen. Sis calls me that, most what know me call me Li'l Al 'cause o' muh daddy. Them what don't know me calls me Tukoolok. That's Eskimo meanin' talks a lot."

Morgan looked at the hotel again, then turned away from it. "I'll call you Took," he said.

Al frowned and then grinned. "That's okay," he said, nodding his approval. "Yessir, that's okay. Jist short for Tukoolok."

"Not quite," Morgan said. "It fits because I think I got took." Morgan ran his hand through the kid's hair. "You follow?"

Al laughed. "No, you follow," he said, and he started down the street with Morgan trailing behind. Morgan liked the boy and he'd rather stay in a private house than a hotel anytime.

5

Li'l Al, or Took, turned out to be Allen Gastineau, second born of Allain Louis Gastineau, one of the founders of the city of Juneau and one of the first white men to set foot in the territories.

Big sister was Micheline and she was all French and all woman. The clothes she wore did little for her femininity but neither could they hide it. She was dark, with almond shaped eyes and skin the texture of maple paste. They talked until near midnight with Morgan, finally turning the conversation to the subject of their father.

"He was one of the founders of Juneau," Micheline said, proudly. "He was the tenth white man to set foot in the territories. He wanted to bring government, law and order to us. He was," she paused and took a breath, "killed, ambushed."

"When?"

"Two years now. He was on his way to Prince Rupert." She looked up and smiled. "That's in British Columbia. His hope was to get some

British assistance from the Mounted Police until Alaska could form its own government and fund its own police."

"Sounds like somebody didn't much care for his idea."

"I wonder."

Morgan looked quizzical.

"It's just that he had so much support and no one knew exactly when he was leaving on that trip and yet they were waiting for him."

When Micheline finally showed Morgan to his room, he found it to be clean, quiet and comfortable. He also realized he was dead dog tired and he laid back and was almost asleep. He was jarred awake quickly.

"Mister Morgan." The voice was Micheline's.

Morgan hadn't realized she was still there.

"I didn't tell you," she said, "but I had a husband. He went off to Dawson in the Yukon eight or nine months back. He got caught in an avalanche." Her dress slipped from the maple hued skin and seemed to float to the floor. "I don't give myself to every boarder but my brother says, you, well, you're different."

Morgan couldn't help but think that Micheline was being pimped by a ten year old, but neither could he resist what stood before him. He'd worry about justifications later.

Micheline's breasts were small, firm and reminded the Idaho gunman of two persimmons. He kneaded them gently and Micheline responded with throaty whispers of "yes" and "good" and "don't stop." He didn't, but instead replaced exploring fingers with an exploring tongue.

The girl's nipples hardened under his ministrations and she seemed to melt onto the bed. Once there, she was at Morgan's mercy and he released weeks of pent up desire upon her.

Micheline's responses seemed to indicate that her previous experiences had been almost totally one sided. No man in her life had apparently ever given her anything, only taken. Morgan's almost frenzied application of his skills heightened his own desire for complete fulfillment.

He positioned her on the bed with her buttocks at its edge, her thighs splayed in a most unladylike position and her arms pinned beneath her by her own weight. She didn't care, she didn't protest, she only closed her eyes and her head was rolling back and forth with each new spot Morgan found.

He let his tongue work its way along the inside of her legs from just above her knees, upwards. He alternated, getting higher each time. There was no change in the girl's response because this had never been done to her before and she could not imagine what was about to happen.

Gently, Morgan spread the folds of flesh reposing just below the silky fine covering of hair. He let his tongue find the moistness near the bottom of the slit and then he moved his head, slowly, upwards. His tongue went back and forth in rapid, short, firm motions. Micheline's breath came in little gasps. "What are you . . . oh, oh. OH . .. AHHHH!"

He struck home. He tightened his grip on her thighs and flicked his tongue faster.

Micheline climaxed, Morgan was certain, for the first time in her life. Her body shook and convulsed with each and every sensation. He stepped back and let her relax after the force of the pleasure. Her leg muscles quivered and jerked spasmodically. Once she had completely drained herself of the event, he leaned down, gently touching her breasts. Her breath immediately returned to short gasps. She opened her eyes, looked at him and smiled.

Morgan slipped his hands beneath her armpits and scooted her up on the bed. He mounted her and now she was anticipating an experience she had known before. He slipped inside her and her hips reared up to meet him, grinding bare flesh against bare flesh.

"Make me finish again, please," she begged, "make it happen again."

He did, careful to tease her clitoris with each thrust and adding the stimulation to her hardened nipples. His efforts had brought him to the very edge more than once and he struggled to stave off a premature release of his own.

They pushed against one another for a very long time, slowly at first, then faster, then slow again, draining from one another all of the pleasure each had to give. Slowly the sensation built until neither of them could restrain themselves any longer. In a single moment, two bodies became one.

The next morning, at the end of Main Street in Juneau, Morgan found the government dock, the packet boat *Golden Gate* and the Eskimo Chotauk. The big Eskimo was inside of a circle of men, eight or nine, and a barrel chested deck hand was circling around him warily. Morgan noted that the sailor had both hands free and held a big Bowie in the right one. Chotauk, by contrast, had only one hand free and no knife.

Morgan eyed the spectators carefully as he

moved nearer to the circle of men. He finally edged between two of them and they glanced at him only briefly. Chotauk spotted him.

"You call it this way?" Morgan asked.

Chotauk shook his head.

The man on Morgan's right suddenly realized that Morgan was an ally of the Eskimo. He reached for his gun. Morgan's was already in his hand but he didn't plan to shoot anybody if he didn't have to, and he didn't. Using the barrel of the Bisley like a club, he smashed it into the man's jaw and sent him reeling. At the same instant, Morgan's left elbow shot back and found the paunch of the man to his left. Morgan followed up on that one and dropped the man with the Colt's barrel laid over the top of his head.

Then he stepped back and cocked the Bisley.

"Now untie the Eskimo's other arm and get rid of the knife."

The man didn't move fast enough and Morgan fired a shot between the man's feet. They were bare.

"You'll lose a toe the next time."

The deck hand complied, tossing the knife aside after he cut the rope binding Chotauk's wrist to his belt. The deck hand eyed Morgan and then his eyes shifted from one man to another around the circle. Suddenly, he found no interest in his plight. Morgan had reholstered the Bisley but none of the sailors were gunmen and they weren't about to test their skill against what they'd already seen.

The deck hand had two brothers and the trio had been charged with unloading the supplies for Mariellen Chapel, under the watchful gaze and direction of Chotauk. They had decided against taking orders from an Eskimo. Two of them quickly realized the error of their judgment, ending up in the water with cooled tempers. The third brother decided on a little more equal match.

Morgan motioned for the circle of men to spread apart somewhat and they did. That done, he nodded. The deck hand moved first and moved fast, spinning around. He charged, bull-like, head down, into Chotauk's middle. The Eskimo grinned, not even grunting. He simply back peddled to keep his balance until he could wrap his huge arms around the man's chest. Once he had locked his fingers together and lifted, the fight was all but over. He continued applying the pressure until the deck hand's face was about the same color as a ripe tomato. Chotauk turned him loose and the deck hand dropped, gasping for breath.

"Need men," Chotauk said to the others. "Five, all work there." He pointed to a cargo net full of crates. "Load onto packet boat, there." He pointed to the mail packet that would be going back up the Taiya Inlet. "Three hours all loaded."

Seven men, not five, answered the call.

Chotauk nodded his head with self satisfaction and then walked over to Morgan. "Chotauk would have won fight. Didn't need help."

Morgan considered him for a moment, smiled, and slapped Chotauk on the arm. "Yeah, I figure you could have, but I thought I'd offer anyhow. You didn't have to take the help if you didn't want it."

Morgan turned to walk away and Chotauk put

a big, meaty hand on Morgan's shoulder and pulled, half turning the gunman around. Morgan frowned.

Chotauk was grinning. "Chotauk like Morgan. You small man with big courage and big gun. Chotauk like Morgan." Chotauk took his hand away and Morgan completed the turn on his own.

This was the first time he'd felt halfway good about Chotauk, but the Eskimo had a postscript to add to his observation. "If you good man to go with courage and gun," he continued, jabbing first Morgan's chest and then his own, "you and Chotauk, we friends." The Eskimo's face suddenly turned hard and he leaned down, close to Morgan's face. "But if you bad man to Lady Boss, you sorry. You fight Chotauk. You shoot Chotauk with big gun and you drown in Chotauk's blood before he die." No further comment was needed.

"Can you handle the rest of the loading?" Morgan asked.

Chotauk nodded.

"I've got a few things to do while I'm here."

"You stay breathing. Lady Boss need Morgan. You die, Chotauk no like."

Morgan looked up, shook his head in despair and smiled. He said, "I wouldn't be too fond of the idea myself Chotauk, and you've just given me another incentive to stay alive. I wouldn't want you on me, even if I was already dead."

Chotauk responded with a broad grin.

Morgan made his way to what constituted downtown Juneau. It was also the territorial capital at the moment and Morgan had government business to attend to. He found his way to the office of the Canadian representative in the territory. The man's name was John R.L.D. Lycoming. He was a stringbean of a man with Lincolnesque features and thick, pure white hair. He gestured Morgan to a seat and then, himself, closed the door. Morgan noted that he stood by it for a few moments, just listening. The action puzzled Morgan but a minute later, Lycoming was smiling, pleasant and all business.

"Welcome to the territories, Mister Morgan."

"Thanks," Morgan replied.

"Your first trip to the land of the midnight sun?"

"I don't know why the hell everyone keep's sayin' that," Morgan said. "In the whole time I've been up here I haven't seen the sun more'n a couple of hours a day."

"Oh, that's because it's gettin' on toward winter. By mid-December you won't see it at all. In the summer the days get longer and longer until the sun never does go down, it just sort of dips. Tell me, what do you think of the place?"

"I haven't formed an opinion, Mister Lycoming. I've been just a bit too busy dealing with some of the less neighborly residents."

Lycoming's expression turned dour, his eyes shifted away from Morgan's face and finally he leaned back in his chair. "Well then, old fellow, what can I do for you?"

Morgan reached into the vest pocket of his buckskin shirt and produced the envelope that had been pushed under his door during the voyage up from San Francisco. He handed it to Lycoming.

"Someone pushed this under my door on the trip up," he said. "There is no postmark, but there is a small red design on the envelope. I was hoping you could tell me what it was."

Lycoming frowned. He eyed the envelope and asked, "The letter, sir, or whatever the contents, didn't tell you anything?"

"There was no letter or anything else. When it was slipped under my door, it was just as you see it now."

Lycoming nodded and then asked, "What brought you here for help?"

"Mail, at least where I come from, is government regulated. This is mail, you're government, and I was told this originated from somewhere in the territory. Territorial mail, I was told, is under Canadian jurisdiction. Was I told wrong?"

"No, no you were not, sir." Lycoming eyed the envelope again, leaned forward and handed it back to Morgan. "In this case, I'm afraid I can't be of much service to you. The red design doesn't indicate where the letter may have been posted."

"Does it tell you anything?"

"Oh yes. Whoever posted it is either in service of, or has access to, the official seal of the Mounted Police." Lycoming reached out and touched the red design with the tip of his finger. "That little stamp is the identification of the RCMP serving the territories."

"This came from the Mounties?"

Lycoming frowned. "Two things, Mister Morgan, in answer to your query. First, we don't call them Mounties. Not up here. Second, I didn't say it came from them, I said whoever placed it in that envelope had access to the stamp."

"Just how easy is that access?"

"Not easy at all old fellow, but there's no assurance that it is official simply because it's on there."

"You've lost me," Morgan said, somewhat irritably.

"The RCMP codes its written communications with a seal or design. Black, for instance, signifies that the point of origin is a regional headquarters such as you might find in Calgary or Edmonton. Green would tell you that the comminque emanated from a district office such as you will find in Prince George, British Columbia. No one would have access to these stamps."

"But the red is different?"

"Different is hardly enough, Mister Morgan. The red is possessed by only a handful of the most experienced field operatives. Men who work in the wilds and take great risks incognito. The only way that you, for instance, would have of coming into possession of the red stamp is by killing the operative to whom it was issued."

"This came from a Mountie, uh, a Royal Canadian police officer who may well have been working out of uniform?"

"That," Lycoming said, "or from the person who killed that officer." Lycoming reached into the top drawer of his desk and removed a file folder. He held it up. "The information is confidential, Mister Morgan, but suffice to say that this folder contains the names of five such operatives, all dead, all killed by person or persons unknown, and all within the past two years. That, sir, is why I can't be of much help to you in your quest."

"I appreciate what help you have given, Mister Lycoming, and I'm working up in Skagway, staying at The Queen's Throne Hotel. If you think of anything else that might be helpful, I'd appreciate knowing about it."

Morgan got to his feet and Lycoming followed suit, extending his hand as he did so. Morgan shook it and Lycoming walked him to the office door and then opened it.

Then, Lycoming spoke again. "There is one other thing you might do, Mister Morgan."

"Yeah? What's that?"

"You might ask yourself the same question I'm asking myself right now."

Morgan looked quizzical. "And what's that, Mister Lycoming?"

"Just what would a special operative for so prestigious an agency as the RCMP want with a second rate American gun fighter?"

There was a time Morgan would have taken the question as an insult but Lycoming was very British, very suspicious about anything American and, for the moment at least, not worth Morgan's time. Nonetheless, Morgan's nature precluded simply ignoring the statement. "I can think of one damned good reason, Lycoming."

The tall man's brows raised. "Really. And what, sir, is it?"

"Maybe he'd like to learn how to stay alive."

6

Mariellen Chapel found Morgan taking his breakfast. She sat across the table from him and he knew at once that she was unhappy. He figured it was probably because he and Chotauk had arrived too late the night before to unload. They had simply put the crates from the packet boat onto wagons and drove the wagons into the storage barn, opting to wait until daylight to unload them.

"You got a beef with me?" Morgan finally asked.

"You do somethin' to give me cause to have a beef with you?"

Morgan grinned. Mariellen seemed to make a habit of answering a question with a question and it was a sure sign she had a beef. He shook his head. "Not as I know of."

"If you'd gone down to Juneau alone, I'd have you shot by now, or sic Chotauk on you. As it is, he already told me that you both kept an eye on the crates all the way back."

Morgan frowned.

"There's not one damn thing in those crates but rocks."

Morgan had a bite of food at mouth level. He paused and then the fork lowered. "You've got enemies aboard the boat up from San Francisco."

"Or at the dock in Juneau, or at the loading docks in San Francisco, or anywhere in between that you can think of."

"Yeah," Morgan said, "and that's a lot of places." He shifted his weight and pushed back from the table, keeping only his coffee cup. "What were you hauling?"

Mariellen considered Morgan carefully. He could tell that she was still uncertain about him. Chotauk had told her everything which had taken place and she knew her uncle put great stock in Morgan's reputation. She also knew, or at least believed, that every man had his price.

"You really don't know?"

"I really don't," Morgan answered. "Should I?"

"Guns."

Morgan leaned forward. "Guns? Nothing but guns?" he asked, incredulous.

"I've been bringing in extra supplies, small amounts of necessities, for months now, building up the stock. It was all so I could have one free load for guns." She rubbed her forehead and cursed under her breath. Mariellen looked up. "Colt pistols. The latest models of the Peacemakers and plenty of ammunition to go with them."

"How many?"

"Fifty."

"Jeezus! Who knew?"

"Me, my uncle and the factory," she paused, "I thought."

"What do you plan, uh, or should I say what *did* you plan to do with fifty Colt Peacemakers?"

"Arm the men I need to hold onto what I've got, Morgan. It's real simple."

Morgan's eyebrows raised and he looked around, gesturing with little bobs of his head. "This place? Fifty men?" He looked into Mariellen's eyes. "It's nice," he continued, "but who in hell wants it that bad? Surely not Skagway Annie?"

"Right church, Morgan," Mariellen replied, "wrong pew. Our problems, mine and hers, are not in Skagway. They're up in Dawson and they're not friendly, they're damned scary."

"What the hell is up in Dawson, more gold?"

"There's gold. Silver too, and copper, and God knows what else Morgan, but our money isn't dug up. It comes from men not mines. They need everything men need and they don't much give a damn who supplies it."

"Look," Morgan said, glancing around to make certain they were still alone, "I'm supposed to be working for you and I'm supposed to be on the outs with your uncle. We both know better. It's Colt I'm really working for," he said. He leaned forward, squinting steely eyes at Mariellen's face and then added, "Isn't it?"

"It is, Morgan, that's the truth of it. They wanted their weapons on the last frontier and they tried the usual methods without success. They finally left it to my uncle to make a deal. He did."

"You're not talking about the deal he has with me, Mariellen. As I see it, I'm an enforcer, nothing else."

"Right again, Morgan. The deal is this. Colt gets a solid foothold in the Klondike and the

Yukon through my uncle and I get all future supplies at special prices because I can purchase them by using the Colt name."

"Sounds like a flim-flam."

"On a smaller scale Morgan, like one little town back down in the states, it would be. In the territories it could mean millions of dollars. Canada, the Mounted Police, all of British Columbia and the rest of Alaska as it opens up." Mariellen leaned back, finished her coffee, put out her cigarette and looked hard. "And it will open up, Morgan, big and powerful and raw and mean but it will open up."

Morgan nodded. He knew she was right. "And Skagway Annie Thompson stands to gain the most if you can't keep your deal, that right?"

Mariellen shrugged. "Who else? We're the two biggest operators in Skagway. No reason for it to be different in Dawson."

Morgan got to his feet. "I've got a little trip to make," he said, smiling and adding, "Lady Boss."

"Morgan," Mariellen licked her lips and swallowed, hard, "be careful."

He nodded.

As he headed for Skagway Annie's place, he mulled over what he had just heard. In many ways, what Mariellen had revealed posed more questions then it answered. On top of that, it was obvious that the lady was scared. He hadn't seen it in her before but there was sure no mistaking it. Morgan began to wonder just how big a game he'd been asked to join. He didn't know yet but he knew one thing for damned sure. No matter how big, he didn't like the hand he was holding.

Morgan reckoned that if Skagway Annie Thompson was behind the theft of the guns, her next move would be to eliminate any possible problems she might encounter with somebody trying to get them back. After her offer to him and his refusal, he seemed the logical target for her efforts. Lee Morgan wasn't a man who liked to sit around and wait for somebody else's next move. If he was supposed to be on the outs with Harrison Chapel and Skagway Annie, he figured he might as well make it look good.

Morgan entered Thompson's Cove and looked at once toward the table where Annie Thompson usually had breakfast. He was either too late or just a shade early. He glanced toward the second floor. One of the two men he'd confronted on his earlier visit stood at the head of the stairs. He was armed with a shotgun. Morgan's eyes met those of the man and this time it was the man who felt safe. The shotgun was cocked and ready and even Morgan's speed wouldn't keep him from a load of shot.

Morgan reached up and tugged at the brim of his hat in a mock gesture of greeting to the man, then he turned on his heel and walked out. The man grinned. Morgan slipped into the walkway between Skagway Annie's place and the only store in Skagway which sold ladies' hats. He caught himself pausing to stare at such an unlikely item as was displayed in the store's window.

Morgan reached the back of Thompson's Cove and found both what he'd expected and what he was looking for. The second man with whom he'd had the earlier run in was now posted outside the second floor doorway. No getting in the backway, in silence anyhow. Morgan had expected it. He also found an outside ground floor window which led into a storage room. Morgan had hoped for it. He knocked out the glass and yanked open the window.

"Who's there?"

Morgan had already stepped back into the walkway. Now he eased forward.

"Who's down there?"

The man had come down about half the stairs. Like his counterpart inside, Skagway Annie's man was armed with a shotgun. Morgan eased forward a little more and then pressed his back against the building and edged around the corner. He was now beneath the wooden stairs and the guard had stopped. Morgan was ready and he tossed an empty bean tin through the broken window.

The man on the stairway acted predictably and took two more steps. As he began the third, Morgan's right hand closed around the man's boot at ankle height.

"Goddam," the man yelled.

He was already pitching forward, face down. He reflexively pulled the trigger on the shotgun and Morgan took advantage of the noise to move back out to the street.

A moment later, the Idahoan eased in the front door and glanced toward the head of the stairs. No man, no shotgun.

"Don't bother, barkeep," Morgan shouted.

The barkeep had not reacted quickly and by the time Morgan reached the top of the stairs, it didn't matter anymore. Morgan's gun was drawn and aimed toward the back bar.

The barkeep, his eyes as big and round as beer mugs, put both hands up and waggled them as he backed slowly away. Morgan smiled and nodded his approval.

"Very good Mister Morgan, but no cigar. Sorry."

Morgan had heard nothing behind him. He whirled. The gun flew from his hand as one of two hulking men in sailor's garb lit in on him. The voice belonged to Skagway Annie and she seemed to be enjoying Morgan's plight.

The smaller of the two men had struck first, knocking Morgan's gun away and then catching the gunman with a solid blow to the mid-section. The second man, much bigger, grabbed Morgan by the collar of his buckskins and whirled him in a half turn. Only Morgan's recuperative skills and his own speed kept the situation from being worse. As it was, he took a solid blow to the jaw and couldn't keep his feet.

Morgan faked a roll to his right hoping to gain a few moments. It didn't work. A third man slipped ham sized hands beneath Morgan's armpits and literally hefted the gunman to his feet, pinning his arms at the same time. The smaller of the two sailors went to work on Morgan's belly at that point. When he finally took most of Morgan's wind and maybe a rib or two, the bigger man moved in and put the lights out with a single, crashing blow to Morgan's jaw.

Morgan sucked in his breath, winced at the pain on his left side, and felt a moment of panic when his hands found solid wood only a few inches from his face. He was on his back.

"Buried alive," Morgan whispered to himself.

A moment later, his hand found open space to his left, then still more. He eased his feet to the left, more space. He was in the confines of a ship's bunk! Shanghaied! He swung himself down to the deck, again wincing with the stabbing pain in his left side. He also instinctively reached for his gun. It wasn't there.

Above him he could hear men's feet on the deck and after gathering his senses and getting his bearings, he also realized they were already at sea! Where? In what direction? How long had he been unconscious? He had to get some answers and he sure as hell wouldn't get them down in the darkened hold of a ship.

His eyes had somewhat adjusted to the darkness but there was damned little light. He did catch enough rays of sunlight for him to determine that it was still daylight. The same day? Now that he couldn't be sure about.

He found a ladder and went up it as far as he could, then put his neck and shoulder to the task of trying to open the deck hatch. It was to no avail. He began pounding on the hatch. He did so, hollering as well, for the next quarter of an hour. No one responded. Morgan found a corner, sat down and wished that he had one of Mariellen's cigareets.

When the hatch finally did open someone was standing at the top looking down at him. It was light outside, but it was the dim light of early morning or late afternoon and all he could see was a silhouette. He tensed, ready to defend himself.

"Morgan, I'm sorry, old boy, but if you'll come up on deck, I'll explain everything."

Chapel? What the hell was going on? Morgan got up, rubbed the back of his head, and moved cautiously to the ladder. Harrison Chapel moved away from the hatch as Morgan ascended slowly and finally emerged. He quickly glanced around, sizing up the deck hands. He was also looking for the trio who'd put him under in the first place. There was no sign of them and the deck hands present all seemed plenty busy.

"Chapel, your niece and I had a talk, uh, damn! How long was I out?"

"You were brought aboard yesterday," Chapel said.

"Yesterday? Yeah, well, as I was saying, Mariellen and I had a talk. I went to do something about it and this is where I ended up. Anyway, she told me a lot I didn't know. I figure the rest of the answers are ones you can supply."

"We have to be careful, Morgan, but consider this. If I didn't plan to give some answers, why would you be here, alive?"

"With all due respect, Chapel," Morgan said, "I've done nothing but answer all sorts of damned questions. Now, I don't plan on going anywhere until I find out just who's sitting in on this little game, and who's staking who."

"I have your weapons and personal things below, Morgan. I did what I did to put the finishing touch to our little charade."

"I don't much care for your approach."

Chapel smiled but at the same time raised his eyebrows at Morgan. "What did you have in mind just before Annie's men jumped you?"

"I'm not sure, exactly," Morgan said, "but I take your meaning. I don't quite understand why you'd go to the trouble you went to and then end up on the same damned boat with me. Isn't that a little risky?"

"It is unless you get dumped over the side in a canvas bag."

"That what you've got in mind?"

"With your cooperation, in the right place at the right time, yes Morgan, I do. I think it would completely free you to do what has to be done."

"Which is?"

"Find out who's against Colt. Who and why."

"Did Mariellen tell me right about the deal with the Colt Company and the battle for Dawson?"

"She did."

"I gather you think that the answer, or answers, to your problems are up in Dawson."

Harrison Chapel shrugged. "In the Yukon territory somewhere, yes." He pooched out his lower lip in an expression of mixed surprise and ignorance. "As to Dawson, I don't know, Morgan. Mariellen tends to be a bit melodramatic at times."

"As far as you're concerned, the trouble could be coming from one of your gun competitors, is that what you think?"

"Why not? Any deal Colt can make, anyone else can make. Can't they?"

"I guess," Morgan said, "if they had the money and the manpower and the contacts."

"There are plenty of all three up here, Morgan."

"How about Skagway Annie? What's her stake in the game?"

"Pretty healthy," Chapel replied, "and there really is no love lost between Annie and my niece but I don't think either of them would have the stomach for murder, outright, if push came to shove."

"Uh huh. Just whose life are you betting on it, Chapel?"

Harrison Chapel considered Morgan for a

moment and then moved again to the hatchway. "Come, I'll show you to your gear and you can get something to eat. I'll join you for some coffee and outline what I have in mind."

"If I'm supposed to be working for Mariellen and I end up supposedly dead, what will she have to do to keep up appearances?"

"It's covered, Morgan," Chapel said, smiling. "She'll be mad, she'll do something to Annie's place, or try. Before it gets too serious, I'll let her in on it."

"You're playing a damned dangerous game, Chapel. You could turn what sounds like a little friendly competition into an all out war."

"Yes, Morgan," Chapel said. "I could, and then supply the guns to fight it to the highest bidder." He gestured below. "Shall we?"

"One more question first, Chapel. What happened to the load of Peacemakers we were supposed to have picked up for Mariellen? We ended up with two crates of rocks." Morgan paused. "Or did you know all of that already?"

"I knew. I aranged it with Colt's. I had to make the first situation look good to, well, uh, you know, whoever is behind this." Chapel looked down. "I wish I could have told you."

Morgan edged past Chapel and went below. When the tall gentleman finally ducked low enough to work into the little room, Morgan had another question ready for him. "You really did make a pretty good show, but where are they?"

Chapel, obviously preoccupied, frowned.

"The pistols you arranged to have stolen."

"Oh yes," Chapel chuckled, "seems like a fair query, Mister Morgan. Well, they are safe, I assure you. They never left San Francisco."

Harrison Chapel moved across the small cabin and fished into a foot locker hidden beneath some woodwork and a blanket or two. From it, he eventually pulled Morgan's gun and holster, possibles he'd been carrying, and the monetary content of his wallet. "Your belongings, Morgan."

Morgan took them in silence, eyeing each with the scrutiny of a man distrustful of everything. This particular plan had smelled sour almost from the beginning. Everything he wanted to check out had proven to be just a little tainted. He was half afraid to check anything, and far too smart not to check everything. Satisfied that his belongings were intact, Morgan turned again to Harrison Chapel.

"Just how realistic a plan do you have in mind for me?"

Chapel grinned. "It will look good, Mister Morgan. I promise you."

Morgan nodded. "I was sure it would. Now, how about reality?"

"You'll find everything you need when we put you ashore, Morgan."

"Since most everybody hereabouts will think I'm dead, or at least hear that I am, just what is everything I need, Chapel?"

Harrison Chapel smiled broadly, walked across the room, slapped Morgan on the upper arm and said, "Transportation my friend, to Dawson, Yukon Territory."

7

The canvas bag was full of body, just as it was supposed to be. Morgan's buckskin outfit and crumpled hat supplied proof of identification. Chapel made certain that the bag was towed in close enough to shore to get caught in the tide. It was found two days later by some fishermen just off the fishing community of Yukulat. The local constable was duly informed.

Morgan had been put ashore some miles away in an isolated bay which led directly into a heavily wooded area near the base of Mt. Fairweather, the highest point in British Columbia. There, Harrison Chapel had promised, transportation would be made available.

Transportation was desperately needed because Morgan was going to have to travel north and east towards Skagway, though he must avoid the town since everyone there, including Harrison's neice, thought he was dead. From there he would bear due north through the treacherous and infamous Chilkoot Pass and into the Yukon territory. He would pass through the tiny settlement of Klukshu and then go east to Whitehorse. After Whitehorse, bearing northwest, Morgan faced two-hundred miles of the most desolate scrub woods in the world. His destination would be Fort Selkirk. Resupplying and resting there, he would then undertake the final leg of his journey, another hundred and fifty miles of desolation, until he reached Dawson.

In Dawson, he was to find a room and await contact from someone known only as B.J.C. Morgan assumed the last initial might stand for Chapel, a third member of the clan, but the consideration was minimal. In his business, and particularly under his present circumstances, assumption of anything could buy him a six-by-six plot of Yukon ice.

But all that was in some distant, undefined future. The first thing he had to do was get there, and for that he would have to use the transportation that was here for him. Too, he would also need equipment and clothing for staying alive under these conditions.

An old Tlingit, with a face that looked like the side of a mountain and legs that seemed to be only half the normal length, took Morgan in tow and showed him to the sled and team he would be using.

The Tlingit took great pride in showing him the sled, a sixteen-foot, basket-type vehicle lashed together with sinews. The runners were of wood, the harness for the dogs of rope and rawhide.

Morgan learned that the rigging had to be just right so the sled would pull even and travel a straight course. He was also shown how to navigate by the stars. He had learned since coming to Alaska that he couldn't count on the sun rising in the east and setting in the west. Here it rose in the west and it set in the west after making a tiny arc of only a few hours across the lower part of the sky. But the moon and stars were exceptionally bright in the crystal night air, and the white glare of the snow made long distance vision possible, even in the middle of the night.

As important as the sled and team would be the equipment he would have with him. An inventory of equipment disclosed the following:

1 lantern
1 gallon of kerosene
1 tarpaulin
1 axe
1 small stove
1 box of matches
1 skillet
1 fur lined sleeping roll
2 woolen blankets
1 large caribou skin
1 Winchester .44-.40
2 boxes .44-.40 cartridges
2 weeks supply of dried deer meat for himself
100 pounds of dried salmon for the dogs

The old Tlingit told Morgan that a caribou skin, placed skin down, was the best thing to use as insulation against the snow. The caribou hairs were hollow and formed an insulation between the snow and the body.

The clothing Morgan would wear was of equal importance to the sled and the equipment he would carry. He was outfitted in a fur parka and pants. He would wear mukluks, which were fur boots made of caribou and wolf.

Morgan started to put on a pair of red

"longhandled" underwear, but the Tlingit stopped him.

"No . . . you wear, you freeze and die."

"What do you mean?" Morgan growled. "I've worn these in Montana winters and they aren't easy winters. These things kept me warm."

"You work with sled, you get hot, you sweat," the Tlingit said. "Then you get cold, sweat freeze . . . you die."

Morgan rubbed his chin and considered what the Tlingit told him. He had learned long ago to listen to the natives . . . be they Apache telling him how to survive on the desert, or Tlingit telling him how to survive in the frozen wastelands.

"All right," Morgan said. "You're the one who knows. The longhandles stay off."

The Tlingit grunted and some of the lines on his face rearranged themselves. It might have been a smile.

There was almost disaster at the very beginning of the trip. With the sled packed and ready, Morgan was about to step onto the runners, when, from out of nowhere, a female wolf appeared. The lead dog, perhaps sexually aroused by the unexpected appearance of pulchitrude in the wild, started after her, pulling the team with him. The old Tlingit made a grab for the sled as it whizzed past him, and managed to jump on. He worked the brake handle and yelled at the dogs at the top of his voice. It took him just a moment to regain control, and a few minutes later he had the sled still, waiting for Morgan to catch up.

"Holy shit," Morgan grunted. "What if they do that while I'm out in the wild?"

"Shoot lead dog," the Tlingit said.

"If I had my way I'd shoot the sonofabitch now," Morgan said. He stepped onto the runners, released the brake as the Tlingit had showed him, and the sled was off like a runaway train.

The temperature was about fifteen below zero.

The old Tlingit trotted along with Morgan for the first couple of hours, sometimes shouting at the dogs, sometimes pointing out things to Morgan to make the sledding easier. Then, when he reached a long, smooth plain where nothing but level snow stretched ahead of him for as far as he could see, the Tlingit grunted something and turned away. Morgan waved at him, then realized that he was all alone.

Morgan had been alone most of his life. He had crossed the most treacherous stretches of desert in the U.S. and Mexico, and he had ridden and packed through the most rugged mountains. But in both cases he had been in his element, working with horses and in the case of the mountains, mules. Dogs were creatures who lay around on the front porch, or by the back door of saloons. They were white, furry little creatures in pink ribbons in the parlors of bawdy houses, or they were slab-sided hounds who ran out to snap at your stirrups when you rode into fly-blown towns. They were even things to eat in some of the Indian villages he had been in . . . but never before had he depended upon them for his very life. But these ten animals running before his sled were his lifeline, and he was damned uneasy about it.

Above and all about him stretched the very universe, overhung with the black curtain of the long, long night, lighted by the moon and the reflected glow from the mantle of snow. Its stark austerity was more awesome than anything he had ever experienced. By comparison, last winter in the mountain cabin seemed like it had been an encampment in the lobby of a downtown hotel. Some might go crazy under such solitude, but Morgan actually found the experience pleasant.

The second day out, Morgan learned that one of the dogs was a shirker. It had simply quit pulling in the harness and leaned back to trot, effortlessly, along. Morgan tried to get the dog to work, but it refused. The Tlingit told him what to do in such a case. An unalterable law up here was that a dog worked, or it was shot. There was no room for a shirker. Reluctantly, Morgan took the dog out of the harness, then shot him.

On the third day, Morgan encountered a stinging wind which whipped up the snow into an artificial blizzard. The wind and snow stung and burned his face so that he could no longer look ahead to where he was going. The Tlingit had told him, however, that the lead dog could find the trail alone. Morgan decided to test the theory and for one entire day he kept his head down, out of the blowing snow, while the lead dog continued the run.

On the fifth day, one of the dogs went vicious. Somehow he managed to chew his way through the harness and once he was free, instead of bounding away into the wild, he suddenly turned and leaped on Morgan, his teeth bared, his eyes red and angry.

The attack was totally unexpected and Morgan was knocked off the sled by the animal. Morgan put up his arm and the thickness of the parka kept the dog's teeth from tearing through to his flesh, though the dog's bite was so strong that it was like having his arm caught in a vise. Morgan rolled in the snow with the dog, all the while reaching for his gun. The draw that was so fast that many a gunman had gone down in the wink of an eye, was now slowed by the fact that he was down, in the snow, and fighting for his life with a would-be killer dog. Finally he got his pistol out, put the barrel under the dog's chin, and pulled the trigger. Blood and brains burst from the top of the animal's head and the vise-grip suddenly relaxed. The animal flopped over in the snow, a fan of red spattered out on the pristine white.

The other dogs reacted to the one gone wild and started snapping and growling at him. Morgan got a length of rope and started after them, beating them until they submitted. After a few well placed lashes, the dogs lay on their bellies with their paws by their noses, looking up through frightened eyes. Once more he was in control.

"All right, let's go," he growled, after he had readjusted the harness. He was down to just eight dogs now. "And no more of this shit. If I have to I'll leave every damned one of you on the trail and walk into Whitehorse pulling the damned sled myself. Now, mush, goddamnit, mush."

8

Morgan had an unaccustomed growth of whiskers when his sled pulled into Whitehorse. Several people turned out to look at him as he arrived. They weren't drawn to him by his appearance . . . dog sleds were common and he had learned enough on this trip to handle the team and sled without calling undue attention to himself. But he had arrived from nowhere, and he had arrived alone. That, in itself, caused some interest.

He was a stranger, and that aroused more interest. Who was he, and what had driven him to the nearly unheard of feat of coming through Chilkoot Pass this late in the year?

Whitehorse may not have been much of a town, but it was a town, with the promise of cooked food, whiskey, and a bed. Morgan decided he would spend a couple of days here. The town didn't seem that much different from Skagway, though Morgan did notice that fewer men seemed to be wearing pistols. That didn't mean they were unarmed, though. Almost everyone he saw was armed, but they were carrying rifles. They had the look of mountain men and prospectors, he thought, not gunmen.

Morgan found a board for the team and a place to park his sled, then he had a look around at the town. He needed a place to stay and he finally settled on a place called the Nugget.

The Nugget was the best place in Whitehorse, a dubious honor considering the other candidates. It was rough hewn of Alaskan timber and the furnishings came from the leftovers. There were no fancy trappings but Morgan concluded that the surroundings were at least on a par with the occupants.

"Howdy mister, and welcome."

Morgan looked up and found himself staring into a cherubic faced girl of about twenty-five. Her hair was coiffed in ringlets and hung down far enough on both sides to frame her face. He guessed her height at about five feet, two inches but nothing else was in proportion.

"Ma'am," he said.

"May I?" She gestured toward a chair as she spoke and Morgan nodded. She held out a lily white, petal soft hand. "I'm Lizzy McCutcheon and this is my place."

Morgan took her hand.

"You must be the fella who come in with the team this morning."

"Word spreads fast."

She smiled. "There are no secrets in Whitehorse, Mister, at least not where strangers are concerned. You bound for Dawson?"

"I can see why there are no secrets," Morgan said, "if you get answers to all your questions."

"I do, one way or another."

"Yeah," Morgan said, "I'm Dawson bound." He

noticed she was eyeing his hands and she glanced toward his hip.

"You're sure as hell no prospector and you wear a piece like you know how to use it." She looked up.

"If I have to use it, I can. I'm no prospector and my business is just that, mine."

"Your handle part o' that business?"

Morgan eyed her. He had agreed with Harrison Chapel to use his father's name, Leslie. As to a first name, Chapel came up with Hank. To Morgan, it made no difference.

"Name's Hank Leslie."

Lizzy McCutcheon motioned for the barkeep and when he reached the table, she said, "I'll have a scotch. Anything else for you, Mister Leslie?"

"Another bourbon."

"These are on me." The barkeep withdrew. "Who you workin' for, Mister Leslie?"

"I told you, I keep my business mine."

"Not up here you won't. Oh, you can keep it quiet for a spell, but as soon as you try to do whatever it is you do, the word will go out. Once it does, the price of your hide goes up."

Morgan looked puzzled.

"It's easy," Lizzy continued, "this land is tough enough for the best of men without having to compete with each other. I figure it would be downright miraculous if you were tryin' to do something somebody else hasn't tried."

"I'm not," Morgan said, "I'm trying to make some money. I can't imagine anybody who hasn't tried that, or isn't trying it right now. No miracles where I'm concerned."

"How would a thousand dollars appeal to you?

Half now and half when you complete the job?"

Morgan's first instinct was to say no but he caught himself. He was supposed to be a man looking to make money. Turning down a chance to do that without at least hearing how would smell a little rotten.

"I don't much care for half payments," Morgan said. "If you don't trust me to do it, you shouldn't ask."

Lizzy McCutcheon grinned. "I agree. I just can't pay you more than I've got and all I can spare from here is half. The other half is up in Dawson at my other place."

"Why'd you pick on me?"

"You're the only man in Whitehorse who's headed to Dawson with an empty sled."

Morgan considered her. "What makes you think it's empty?"

"I knew it was empty fifteen minutes after you got into town and at least that much before you walked in here. Most men peddlin' somethin' got goods. You got nothin' except what you need to get to Dawson and up here that's a damned sin."

"A sin?"

Lizzie nodded. "Need a lot up north. Man ought not go empty handed."

Morgan eyed the girl and then leaned back and said, "That seems like a fair amount of money for one sled full of supplies."

"It's ten percent of the value of what you'll be hauling for me."

"Which is?"

"Now that's my business, Mister Leslie. Isn't it?"

"Not if I'm hauling it," Morgan said. "I figure you approached me because you spotted me for a gun hand, not a prospector. You're hiring my gun, not me." Morgan looked around. "There's a dozen men in here right now who know the country better and know everything there is to know about a sled and team. Unless you figure on trouble, one o' them would already be on the trail."

The girl got to her feet, scooted her chair back under the table and then said, "I'll buy you a venison steak this evenin' Mister Leslie, and we'll talk some more. We can both decide after that. Seven o'clock suit you?"

"I don't recollect any better offers since I hit town. Seven's fine."

Morgan watched the girl walk away and his mind shifted from her offer to the sway of her hips. It was a hell of a long ways to Dawson and fresh memories were about the only company he could imagine having on the trail.

"That was good," Morgan said, wiping his mouth. He tossed the napkin aside and took a swallow of coffee. "I never much cared for deer meat but that was good."

"You learn lots o' things about cookin' in this country," Lizzie said, "when you don't have much to work with. One day, I plan to try to bring in some honest to God beef."

Morgan frowned. Lizzie's comment stirred a faint memory. "Seems to me that somebody tried that once."

"So I've heard," Lizzie said, "gent from Wyoming a few years back." She laughed. "He got paid well enough, that's sure, but he never lived to spend it."

"Runnin' cows in this country would be next to impossble."

"Nothin' is impossible Mister Leslie, unless them what tries it don't believe it. He got the cows here, he just didn't have any plans after that."

"Speaking of plans, I'd like to know what yours are for me."

"Upstairs, Mister Leslie," Lizzie replied, getting to her feet, "and I'll do better than tell you, I'll show you."

Morgan considered her, looked around the room, and realized that no one was paying them any mind. He nodded and stood up.

Lizzy McCutcheon's room was pleasant, warm and feminine with the low notes of her perfume hanging in the air like an invitation. The bed was a big four-poster, hand hewn like the rest of the furniture, but by a craftsman who took pride in his work. In addition to the bed there was an overstuffed chair, a rocker, a fine china cabinet, and a spinet. Morgan took the overstuffed, tossing his hat onto a straight back chair nearby.

"Do you like wine, Mister Leslie?"

"Good wine, yes."

Lizzie poured two glasses and handed one to him. The color was a deep, rich burgandy, glowing as if it had captured inner fire. Morgan sniffed it, then tasted it, and found it was as good as any he had drunk in San Francisco.

When she saw the expression of surprise on his face she smiled. "I do what I can to make life bearable up here," she said. She sat on the edge of the bed. "I've got three big wooden crates in a storeroom downstairs, Mr. Leslie. They're full of dynamite."

"Dynamite?"

"As you might imagine with all the prospecting and mining going on up here, that's one of the most precious commodities in the territories."

"I can see that," Morgan said. "I can also see that it might be difficult to hang on to something like that."

"Hard enough," Lizzie said. "I haven't tried to ship it yet because of that very thing. There are people who will try and get it, and they don't give a damn how they do it. That's where you come in."

"The job seems to be worth a little more than a thousand dollars," Morgan said. Their eyes met. "Wouldn't you agree?"

"Yes," she said, pausing, "but there is a bonus."

"A bonus? Like what?" Morgan asked.

"Like me," Lizzie replied.

Morgan wasn't disappointed. His imagination had, if anything, underestimated what was hidden beneath the unflattering clothes. Indeed, little else was in proportion to Lizzie's height. Her breasts were full and firm, and the hue and texture of her skin was that of a woman much younger. Morgan had bedded many women half the age of Lizzie who had less to offer.

Lizzie took the role of aggressor and did so with zeal and class. She didn't flaunt herself like a whore, but neither was she the timid housewife who only made love once a week, on her back, after a bath.

Lizzie explored Morgan's muscular body, first with her fingers, and then with her lips. She advanced quickly to her tongue after determining his most sensitive areas. The Idaho gunman relaxed and let nature and Lizzie take their respective courses.

She found his considerable manhood and

began a sensual stroking of it, first with tongue, then with her hand and then a combination of both. He was quickly aroused but she positioned herself so that she could control any involuntary movement.

Each time Morgan tried to respond with a touch or reaction of his own, Lizzie bore down her weight and stopped him. She wanted to give, not receive. Morgan finally accepted the situation and succumbed. Lizzie McCutcheon had both a sense of what a man liked, and a feel for just how far to go with it. Several times, Morgan was certain that she was about to take him to a climax, but each time she stopped and left him hanging in space, breathing hard, completely vulnerable.

After several times like this, Lizzie suddenly got up. "Now," she said, "give me what I want." She moved to the end of the bed, reached out and grasped the posts with each hand, then bent forward from the waist. At the same time, she planted her feet wide apart. Morgan needed no further coaching or invitation. He was rock hard and ready.

He bent his knees slightly and carefully inserted himself into Lizzie's depths, now well lubricated with her own juices. She moaned as she felt him make the insertion. He steadied himself with a small adjustment in his own position and then he began to thrust, slowly. At the same time his hands went down to grasp her breasts. He fingered the nipples and Lizzie moaned again. He stroked and kneaded them.

"Oh, God, yes, that's it, yes! That's what I like. Do it! Don't stop, keep doing it. Do it for both of us."

Morgan did it for both of them, for a very long time.

"Finish it this way," she moaned.

Morgan did finish it that way in a sudden, gushing burst of sperm and sensation. Lizzie's whole body stiffened and even in his own passion, Morgan could sense Lizzie's climax and her juices released. She was, he thought, a different kind of woman. She climaxed almost like a man.

When it was over, Morgan slipped from her, but he continued kneading her breasts and kissing her bare back, working down her smooth skin until he could gently kiss her buttocks. She sighed and swayed gently, but made no protest to his post climax display. He finally straightened and stepped back and Lizzie stood up and turned around. She stepped up to him, pressing her nakedness against his own. Kissing him, she stepped back and said, "I was wrong, Mister Leslie."

"Wrong about what?"

"I promised you a bonus. But it was I who got the bonus."

Morgan returned her smile. All this, he thought, eyeing her, and class as well.

If every other facet of his makeup was lost during the lovemaking process, Morgan's thinking processes remained ever sound, ever searching. Something was bothering him and it finally surfaced.

"Did I hear you right?" he asked, pulling on his boots. "Did you say my fee was ten percent of the value of what I was hauling?"

Lizzie, still dressing, turned to face him. "That's what I said. Damned expensive dynamite, isn't it?"

Morgan stood up. "Yeah, even up here I'd say ten thousand dollars is damned expensive dynamite."

"There are two commodities in very short supply in this country, Mister Leslie. Dynamite and handguns. If you have dynamite, you'll need handguns to protect it. If you have handguns, you've got to figure a way to get them where they're needed, without losing them."

"Wait a minute. Are you telling me you have pistols in this load? Pistols packed in dynamite?"

His face became stern, but before he could pursue the matter, Lizzie replied. "Who'll bushwhack a load like that and risk losing both?" Lizzie smiled confidently at her own query. It smacked of a certainty.

Morgan wasn't so sure. "What make of hand guns?" he asked.

Lizzie looked puzzled that he would ask such a question. "Remingtons. Why?"

"Well, if I was working for, say, Colt Firearms, this kind of shipment would be made to order for me. I wouldn't give a damn about blowing up a load of dynamite and my competitor's handguns with it." He strapped on his rig and tied down the holster. When he looked up, Lizzie was still considering his last observation.

"You're suggesting that representatives of these gun manufacturers, men who have to have government clearance to even come up here, would go to such lengths?"

"I've never known greed to be picky about who it infects, and with what's at stake in this country, I don't know many men whose resistance is that high."

"But the territorial government restricts American gun sales. And every representative has to undergo a full investigation of his background."

"So I understand," Morgan replied, smiling, "but who investigates the investigators? Are you trying to say that the investigators are so noble and fine that they can't be tempted if enough money is waved in their face?"

"My God! I never considered the possibility. The raids, the murders, the trouble we've been having, it could have been—" she let the sentence dangle as she paced across the room. She turned back and looked at Morgan with a troubled expression on her face. "I just figured it was locals trying to horn in on the market."

"Tell me, how do you manage to deal in guns?" Morgan thought about his question, then added, "Legally, I mean."

"I was the first business in Whitehorse to make the request. I went through weeks of filling out forms, answering questions from RCMP people, everything it took. I had no competition to speak of, but even that didn't assure me of a license."

"You got those Remingtons legal then?"

"Legal as hell, Mister Leslie. And very costly. I'll lose my ass if those guns are bushwhacked."

"Yeah? Carrying guns packed in dynamite, I may literally lose my ass before this is all over," Morgan said.

"I . . . I guess I didn't think of that," Lizzie said. She brushed her hair back with her hand. "It's just that the situation is critical right now."

"You must be pretty desperate to select a total stranger and then tell him everything. You don't know me," Morgan said, moving a little closer, then adding, "or do you?"

"I don't," came the quick reply. "And I can't afford the luxury of getting to know you. You're a gamble, Mister Leslie, a crap shoot. I'm out of time." Lizzie McCutcheon then made a statement which, under other circumstances, would have caused Morgan to burst into laughter. "Hell," she said, "for all I know you could be working for the Colt Firearms Company."

Morgan didn't respond to her observation. Instead he asked, "Who's your contact with Remington?"

"Fella by the name of Parmenter. Oliver Parmenter. I checked on him myself," she said. "I mean, besides what the RCMP and the territorial government did. He's legitimate."

"And your buyer in Dawson?"

Lizzie grinned. "Now him, I got no worry 'bout, Mister Leslie. He's been up there, so some say, since the first day of creation. He's half Eskimo and half polar bear. Fella by the name of Crowder. Big Ben Crowder."

Morgan's mind clicked. His contact in Dawson was someone with the initials B.J.C. Crowder . . . Ben Crowder. "What's his middle name?"

Lizzie wrinkled her brow and nose in a look of complete puzzlement, then she laughed. "Hell, Mister Leslie, I don't know. It was only three months ago that I found out Big Ben had a last name."

"Is he the only buyer in Dawson?"

"Only one I've got, and the only one I know anything about."

"Then he'd be a buyer from anyone coming in with a load of guns, no matter the make. That right?"

"I reckon it is, but Big Ben is honest. He wouldn't play both ends against the middle. If I show first, he buys from me. If Colt or somebody else shows first—" Lizzie shrugged.

"Why are you so certain about this fella, Big Ben?"

Lizzie McCutcheon played her ace. "My daddy was not much of a man. Too much whisky, too little backbone. Ever' shortcomin' he had was reason to hit my mama, and he had a lot of short-comin's. He did it once too often, I guess. I only know what I heard. I reckon I was about two years old. Anyway, Mama grabbed me an ran, an' daddy was hot after her, and they both run headlong into Big Ben. When it was over, Daddy was dead and mama was grateful."

Lizzie walked right up to Morgan now, and looked him straight in the eye. "Big Ben Crowder is my step daddy, Mister Leslie."

9

Lee Morgan had been in tight spots before. Hell, he'd lived most of his adult life moving from one tight spot to another, but this particular one rubbed and chafed and raised welts everywhere. He was supposed to have gone to work for the Colt people, but he didn't. He ended up working for a hellion named Mariellen Chapel. He was supposed to have a feud going with her uncle, but he didn't. Now, he was supposed to be dead, but he wasn't. And topping off the whole thing was a new job for another hellion named Lizzie.

When Morgan left Whitehorse, he had a lot more confidence in his ability as a musher. He had been taught the most basic elements of the craft by the Tlinget Indian, but he had actually learned from the best teacher of all, experience. Having spent two weeks on the trail with nobody or nothing to depend on but his own skills, he was now as comfortable on the runners of the sled as he would be on the seat of a wagon. Hell, there was nothing about dog teaming that a reasonably intelligent, well coordinated, physically fit man couldn't handle. Morgan fit all those requirements, so dog sledding became routine for him.

On the third day out when he figured he was no more than a couple of hours from Dawson, Sheba, his lead dog, suddenly pulled up. Her snout went up in the air, she pawed, she growled, then she died. At almost the same instant the dog next to her rolled to his right as the bullet that had just killed Sheba ripped into his right, front shoulder. By the time the sound of the first shot carried to him, another dog was down.

The Idaho gunman didn't waste time trying to figure out what was going on. He might be in the frozen wastelands of the Yukon, but he had been under fire enough times to have already picked out the true sound of the rifle from the many echoes that were reverberating back from the low scrub trees. He grabbed his Winchester and, crouched low, ran, hell bent, for a low lying spiny ridge of ice and rock about fifty yards off to his left. Oddly enough, no one bothered to even shoot at him. They were after his dog team and he heard yelps of pain and surprise from the animals as one by one they were taken down by hidden riflemen.

When Morgan reached the scanty security of the ridge and dived over it, he had counted three separate rifles in action. That meant there were at least three men out there, maybe more. He turned around and looked back toward his team. By now all ten animals, including the two replacements he had picked up in Whitehorse, were down. He could see a widening pool of blood as the animals bled their life out on the snow, betrayed by the humans they were trained to serve.

"Sonofabitch!" he swore softly.

He couldn't see a damned thing, but he knew that whoever was out there had to be pretty good shots. They had taken out his entire team and he was certainly a bigger target than any of the dogs. He also knew he wouldn't be going anywhere for a spell, and when he did go, it would be on foot. The guns and the dynamite he could forget about. Whoever was behind this attack was playing for keeps, with no concern about life, either human or animal.

"Hey, mister!" one of the assailants called. "Mister, iffen you'll throw down that rifle we seen you pick up, an' walk up to the sled with your hands up, we'll let you get some food an' water. You can make it into Dawson on foot iffen you got some supplies."

Morgan didn't answer.

"All we want's what's on the sled," one of the others called.

Still no answer.

"This here's rough country," the first assailant yelled again. "You ain't gonna survive 'lessen we let ya'."

"All right, you bastards," Morgan whispered, "it's your territory and it's rough. But rough is rough, whether it's up here or back where I come from. I'll just wait you sonofabitches out."

"Mister? You gonna take us up on our offer?"

Morgan raised up as the last man was calling and he saw what he was looking for, the little wisp of vapor that came from the hardcase's mouth, drifting over the rock and purpling in the dim light of the sun, setting now after its brief sojourn across the sky.

"You know what I think?" Morgan shouted back. He levered a round into his Winchester and pointed the rifle toward where he had seen the vapor.

"What do you think?" the vapor asked.

"I think you can go to hell." Morgan drew a bead and waited. He knew the sonofabitch would raise his head to have a look and that was all he needed, just a split second.

A head raised up above the rock, just far enough for the eyes to look over the top, though since he was wearing a parka, the eyes couldn't be seen. Morgan put the front blade sight of his rifle even with the gate sight at the rear, and right in the middle of the shadow of the parka hood where he imagined the eyes were. He let out half his breath, then he squeezed the trigger.

The rifle barked and kicked back against his shoulder and he saw a little mist of blood spew out of the dark shadow. The man fell to his left, flopping out into the snow with arms akimbo. Morgan knew he had killed him with one shot.

"Holy shit! Did you see that?"

"Shut up, you stupid bastard. It was a lucky shot."

"Carter? Carter, where are you? Do you see 'im?"

Morgan heard the heavy bore boom of a big Sharps .50. The bullet crashed through the snowy spine in front of him, taking out a chunk of ice the size of a man's head. This was a new player in the game. He had spotted the other three men, but this one he knew nothing about. The thing that shocked Morgan the most, however, was that the bullet came from the rear! Carter, whoever he was, was behind him.

Morgan couldn't stay here. The man with the Sharps had his range. The next bullet would find its mark and with a .50 caliber it didn't much matter where he was hit. Even a leg wound could kill him out here. Morgan got up and started running. The two smaller rifles across the way opened up on him. Morgan clutched his gut, spun once, then fell.

"I got 'im! I got the sonofabitch!" one of the men yelled excitedly.

"You got 'im? What do you mean you got 'im? I had a bead right on 'im."

"Hell, maybe we both got 'im."

No one got me, you bastards, Morgan thought. At least, not yet. Morgan, who was unhit, eased his head out of the snow and peered toward the sled. The two men from the other side of the clearing were moving toward it. He could hear the third man, the one with the Sharps, coming up from behind him, his boots crunching through the crust of the snow.

"Carter? Roll 'im over, Carter. See'f he's got two bullet holes in 'im or just mine."

Morgan looked toward the sled. The two men were almost there, the third was on him. Morgan waited until he felt the boot on his side. He felt the pressure as Carter rolled him over to check for bullet holes. Morgan rolled over on his back and smiled up at Carter.

"Surprise," Morgan said.

"What the hell?" Carter shouted. He tried to raise his big Sharps into firing position but he was a trifle slow. Morgan's pistol cracked and Carter died, clutching at the sudden hole in his neck.

"Jesus!" one of the two men at the sled shouted.

Morgan grabbed his rifle and rolled once in the snow, levering a shell into the chamber as he did so. At almost the same time the two men at the sled fired and their bullets came so close that Morgan felt a sting of snow in his face from the near miss.

Morgan rolled over onto his stomach, then, from the prone position, fired at the black, bulging blob that was his sled.

Craaaack! The rifle spit out its missile, and almost at the same moment there was a bright red-orange flash, followed by the shock wave and stomach shaking boom of an explosion.

Morgan covered the top of his head with his arms and buried his face in the snow as debris began raining back down from the explosions. He felt the stinging impact of dozens of tiny pieces falling on him, though there was not one piece of anything large enough to do more than sting.

When the final echo was but a rumble, like far-away thunder, Morgan raised his head and looked over to where the sled had been. The snow was scattered with black objects . . . pieces of sled, pieces of guns and the crates the guns were packed in, and most gruesome of all, pieces of the two men who had been standing over the sled.

Morgan looked down at the body of the one the others called Carter. Carter's eyes were wide open but they had already taken on the glazed look of death. His hands were still clutched over the hole in his neck and the blood was already congealed, moments away from being frozen.

Morgan looked through Carter's pockets.He found one-hundred dollars in ten dollar bills, but nothing else. A check of the first man he killed disclosed the same thing . . . one-hundred dollars in ten dollar bills, but nothing else. Morgan looked around on the snow for a few minutes, then found what he was looking for. A ten dollar bill. Then another, and another after that until he managed to recover an additional 120 dollars, all in ten dollar bills. He also saw the charred remains of a couple of bills.

"Well, gentlemen," he said to the men who had ambushed him. "It would seem that you were paid one-hundred dollars apiece to steal my load. Now that you've had time to think about it, do you think it was worth it?"

With $320 more than he started the trip with, Morgan decided to go on into Dawson. He wasn't looking forward to the long walk, then he happened to think of the men who had ambushed him. They sure as hell didn't walk out here. How did they get here?"

Morgan followed their tracks for a short distance, then he found their horses. Smiling, he mounted one, then turned the others free.

"You want to come back in town with me you can," he said. "But I'll be damned if I'm going to lead you."

As if they understood, the horses followed obediently along. Morgan returned to the dog sled trail. The horse was sure footed and used to the snow. The last part of his trip to Dawson was a breeze.

10

After several days in the wilderness, the appearance of Dawson was quite a contrast. A booming little city of ten-thousand people, Dawson had fifteen saloons, five bakeries, two laundries, twelve general merchandise stores, fruit, cigar and confectionary stores, a meat market, a printing shop, four hotels, six restaurants, two bathouses, two barbershops, a hospital and a bank.

The appearance of the bank gave Morgan an idea. The ten dollar bills he found on the bush-whackers were American. Surely a bank in the Yukon, part of the Canadian Northwest Territories, would be able to tell him who had drawn four-hundred dollars in American currency. He stopped in front of the bank, swung down from the horse, and went inside.

The bank was well lighted and busy. In addition to the tellers' cages, there was an asseyor's desk for gold, and a land claims desk. Two wood burning stoves roared in the center of the room and Morgan, who had been cold for three weeks, walked over to stand by one of them for a moment. A few people looked at him as they entered or left the bank, but no one gave him a lookover that he would characterize as unusual. There were so many prospectors being drawn to the Klondike by the promise of gold that one more new face in the crowd aroused no abnormal curiosity.

When Morgan felt the warmth beginning to come back to his fingers and hands, he stepped away from the stove, then went up to the window marked currency exchange.

The man behind the window had thin,blond hair and rimless glasses. He looked up at Morgan. "American for Canadian, or Canadian for American?" he asked.

"Canadian for American."

"How much?"

"Four-hundred dollars."

"The exchange is $440 Canadian for $400 American." The clerk started to count out $400, counting it out in ten dollar bills. Morgan took $440 of the Canadian money he had been paid by Lizzie, and counted out for the exchange.

"Have you made this exchange before?" Morgan asked.

The clerk pointed to the sign over his window. "Currency exchange, that's what I do," he said. "Of course I've done this before. Do you think I don't know the exchange rate?"

"No, that's not what I mean," Morgan said. "What I mean is, I'm looking for someone . . . someone who might have made this exact exchange in the last few days . . . $440 Canadian for $400 American."

"That's not an unusual amount," the clerk said. He finished counting out the bills, then took the money from Morgan. "Will there be anything else?"

"No," Morgan said. He put the money in his pocket, then left the bank. So much for that piece of detective work. It got him absolutely nowhere.

When he stepped out front, he saw someone looking very closely at the horse he had ridden in on, the horse that had belonged to one of the ambushers.

"Something about that horse interest you, mister?"

"What? No, no, I was just admirin' him, that's all."

"Where's the livery?"

"Right down the street."

"Thanks."

Morgan rode the horse down to the livery, dismounted, then led the animal inside. He was met by a short, round man, bald on top, but with a bushy white beard.

"Board your horse, mister?"

"Yeah, I guess. You the only livery in town?"

"The only honest one," the man said. "They's a few folks claim they can board 'an keep your horse for you in a lean-to they got behind their shanty. I wouldn't count on 'em iffen I was you." The stableman looked at the horse pretty close, then looked at Morgan. Morgan saw in his eyes that he recognized the horse.

"You know this horse, do you?"

"I reckon I do."

"Whose horse is it?"

"Mister, you tell me it's yours an' board 'im here, far as I'm concerned, it's yours."

"It's not my horse," Morgan said. "I found him on the trail comin' up from Whitehorse. I'd like to know who he does belong to."

The hostler rubbed his whiskers and stared at the horse for a long moment. "Well, sir, he was rode into Dawson by a fella the name of Carter Lane. But from what I observed of Mister Carter Lane, that don't mean he owns the horse . . . it just means he rode 'im in."

"You're not givin' this fella, Carter Lane, a very high recommendation," Morgan said.

"I wouldn't want him guardin' my hen house," the stableman said. "Iffen I take the horse, who'll be payin' his fare?"

"What's the boarding fee?"

"Five dollars a day. That includes his feed."

"Five dollars a day? My God, I could stay in the finest hotel in San Francisco for five dollars a day."

"You ain't in San Francisco, mister, an' this animal don't eat frozen salmon. He eats hay an' oats an' ever' ounce has to come up the Yukon River, an' that means they ain't nothin' come up since the first week of October, an' there ain't nothin' else gonna come up 'till the middle of May."

"That's five bucks Canadian, I hope," Morgan said, remembering the unbalanced exchange rate.

"Yeah, Canadian," the liveryman said with a broad, yellow toothed smile.

Morgan counted out twenty dollars. "I'll come back before this runs out to let you know if I'm gonna keep him here any longer. Say, you don't know anybody who runs with this fella, Carter Lane, do you?"

"No, but try over at the North Star Saloon. I seen Lane over there a few times."

"Thanks," Morgan said.

He started to turn when he suddenly saw something in the liveryman's eyes, a widening of the pupils, a narrowing of the lids. There was a barely perceptible quickening of the liveryman's breath.

"Uh, yeah, be seein' you," the liveryman said. The tone of his voice was half a pitch higher, as if his throat had involuntarily contracted.

Over the years, Morgan's survival had been dependent upon his ability to interpret and use every sensory input. Many thought the Idaho gunfighter had a sixth sense, and in that he had an exceptional ability to use the five normal senses, one could almost say that he did have a sixth sense. That came into play now, for he knew that someone was behind him, and he knew that someone was about to try to kill him. Morgan took one step to the left, then hurled his body to the right. The would be killer's gun roared even as Morgan was in mid-air. The bullet hit the wood of the nearest stall, sending splinters flying. The horse neighed and reared up in fear, while the liveryman dived for cover. As all this was happening, Morgan twisted around so that he could see the assailant. By the time Morgan hit the ground, he had his Colt in his hand.

"You sonofabitch!" the bushwhacker yelled.

Morgan saw him move the gun toward him, saw him thumb the trigger back for a second shot. He never got the second shot off, for Morgan's own pistol was blazing then, and his bullet caught the hardcase right in the breastbone. The impact of the bullet knocked the hardcase through the door of the livery, out into the hard packed snow of the street. He fell in a pile of horse turds; then, his feet still working, he pushed himself on his back for a few feet as if that way he could escape.

Morgan was back on his feet instantly and he hurried over toward the wounded man with his gun out in front of him. He kicked the wounded man's gun away, then, satisfied that there wasn't another weapon available to the man, he holstered his own pistol and looked down at his victim.

Blood was bubbling out of the hole in the man's chest, and Morgan could hear the wound sucking air. Morgan dropped to one knee beside the man.

"Why'd you try to bushwhack me?" he asked.

The man coughed. "You . . . you go to hell," he said.

"You're dyin', mister," Morgan said. "It can't matter to you now. Who are you? Why did you try to kill me just now?"

The man coughed again. "I needed a grubstake," he said. "I got a hunnert dollars to do this."

"Who gave it to you? Who, man?"

"The mountie," the man said.

"The mountie?"

"Yeah, you know. The Canadian law." The man broke into a coughing seizure. "I mean, he ain't wearin' that red suit or nothin', but he's a mountie, I seen the papers."

"But why?" Morgan asked. "Why would a mountie pay you to kill me?"

"He said you was wanted by the Canadians, said they was a price on your head. I'd get a hunnert now an' the reward when he told headquarters."

"Who is this mountie? What's his name?"

The man reached up and grabbed Morgan's arm, then squeezed it hard. "Mister," he said. "I got me a terrible hurt in my gut. It's . . ." He dropped his arm, his head rolled to one side and his eyes stared ahead blankly. The sucking sound in his chest stopped.

Morgan stood up. By now there were two or three dozen men gathered around, looking down at the dead man. More were coming down the street, materializing out of the dark. He could hear them talking quietly as they approached.

"Anybody know this fella?" Morgan asked.

"Figured you must," one of the men said. "You killed him."

"Never saw him in my life 'till he opened up on me," Morgan said.

"That there's the truth," the liveryman said. "I seen it all. This fella on the ground come sneakin' up behind this man. Next thing you know they was both blazin' away at each other. Onliest thang I don't know is how you know'd he was there," the liveryman said.

"You told me," Morgan said.

"Mister, you must be loco. I never told you a goddamned thang."

"Who is it?" Morgan asked again.

"The only thing I ever heard him called was Sourdough Mike," someone said. "He mostly stays out prospectin', he don't get into town much."

"He should'a stayed out there," someone else said.

"Out of my way. Out of my way, please," an authoritative voice was saying.

As the people parted to let the new man pass,

Morgan saw the red coat and black trousers of a Northwest Mounted Policeman. The policeman looked at Morgan, then pointed to the dead man. "Are you the cause of this?"

"You might say that."

"I'll take your gun." The mountie held his hand out.

"I'm not ready to do that just now," Morgan said.

"Mister, I am ordering you to surrender your gun to me."

Morgan looked at the policeman and smiled. The policeman not only didn't have a gun in his hand, the flap over his holster was snapped down so that anything close to a quick draw was absolutely impossible. And yet he had *ordered* Morgan to turn over his weapon.

"Now how the hell do you think you can make that order stick?" Morgan asked.

"I can make it stick because I have the authority of the law behind me," the policeman said. "Now please hand over your pistol to me, sir, or stand arrested for resisting the law."

"Constable, I can tell you, this here fella was just defendin' himself," the liveryman said. "The man layin' there come up behind him with no word o' warnin' or nothin'."

"If that is the case, you will be released to your own recognizance in a very short time. Provided you offer no resistance now."

Morgan thought about it for a moment. "Constable, I want you to know this is the second time today someone's tried to bushwhack me, and I don't know why. So you can see I'm not too keen on givin' up my gun."

"You will be in my custody," the constable

said. "And under my protection. No one would dare assault you while under custody of the law."

Morgan sighed, then handed his gun over with a wry smile. "Now, why doesn't that make me feel safe?" he asked.

"Come along," the constable said, sticking Morgan's gun down in his belt. He waved his arm at the crowd. "Give way, here, give way," he said. "Give way in the name of the law."

11

Constable Edmond Bannister returned Morgan's pistol.

"I've checked your story, Mr. Leslie," he said. "There was another witness in addition to the liveryman and he verified what happened. You are free to go."

"Thanks," Morgan said, buckling his pistol around his waist.

The constable tossed a few chunks of wood into the little stove, then held his hands over the top. He eyed Morgan carefully. "We don't see too many gun rigs like that up here," he said. "Are you an American gunfighter?"

Normally, when someone called Morgan a gunfighter, he made some deferential statement. But this wasn't a statement of accusation, nor was it the utterance of a thrill seeker. Constable Bannister was a no-nonsense lawman, asking a sensible question. Maybe, if Morgan was frank with him, he would be helpful to Morgan.

"Yes," Morgan said with a sigh. "I am what you might call a gunfighter."

"I see," the constable said. "And why are you

in Dawson?"

"Constable, I don't know what you know about gunfighters," Morgan said.

"Not too much, I'm afraid. But from what I do know, I don't think I'd care to know one."

"There are some who hire their guns out to the highest bidder," Morgan said. "They market their skill and they don't care who buys them."

"Are you telling me you aren't like that?"

"Yeah," Morgan said. "I'm telling you I'm not like that."

"But you do hire your guns." It wasn't a question, or even an accusation. It was a statement of fact.

"Yes, I hire my guns. But I've never killed a man who wasn't trying to kill me. I don't live with the ghosts, Constable."

"Would you care for some tea, Mr. Leslie?"

Morgan would rather have been offered coffee, but anything hot would taste good now.

"Yes, thanks. By the way, my name isn't Leslie."

"Oh?" The Constable looked up at him as he poured two cups of tea. "Isn't that the name you gave me?"

"That's the name I was going by," Morgan said. "My name is Morgan . . . Lee Morgan."

"Lee Morgan?" The constable walked over to his file cabinet and rummaged through a few papers, then picked one up and looked at it. "Mr. Morgan, according to the information I have, you are supposed to be dead. You were abducted from Skagway and your body washed ashore near Yukalat."

"That wasn't me," Morgan said.

The constable took a swallow of his tea and

studied Morgan over the rim of his cup for a moment. Finally he spoke. "Would you care to tell me the story?" he asked.

"I will, I'll tell you everything," Morgan said. "But first, I would like to ask a few questions, if you don't mind."

"All right. I'll answer what I can."

"First of all, the man I killed tonight. . ."

The constable smiled and held up his hand. "This afternoon," he said. "It was only half past three when you shot him. The darkness is confusing to new people."

"Yeah," Morgan said. "Yeah, I been up here a couple of months now and I'm still not used to it. Anyway, the man I killed told me he had been paid one-hundred dollars to kill me."

"I see. And did he say who paid him this money?"

"He said he was paid by the mountie."

Constable Bannister knitted his eyes together.

"The mountie?"

"That's what he said."

"Good heavens, did he tell you I was the one who paid him?"

"No. He said it wasn't a uniformed mountie. He said it was someone else. Supposedly, I am wanted by the Canadian law."

"No, Mr. Morgan, you are not wanted by the Canadian law, neither as Lee Morgan, nor as Hank Leslie. That part of his story is patently false, as is the part that he was contacted by a member of the Northwest Mounted."

Morgan reached in his pocket and pulled out the envelope that had been pushed under his door during the voyage up to Skagway. He handed the envelope to Constable Bannister.

"Does this mean anything to you?"

The constable looked at the envelope for a moment, then looked up at Morgan. "Is this it?" he asked. "An empty envelope, no address, no postmark?"

"This is it," Morgan said. "It was pushed under my door just as you see it."

"The red seal is an official seal," Bannister said. "And it is the seal of the plainclothes officers who—" Bannister stopped and looked at the seal more closely. Then he pulled open the middle drawer of his desk and took out a magnifying glass. He examined the seal closely through the glass. "Damn," he muttered.

"What is it?" Morgan asked.

The constable motioned Morgan over, then held the glass over the seal.

"Look in the upper right hand corner of the seal," he said. "Do you see the break in the line there?"

"Yes."

"Timothy McCutcheon."

"What?"

"This seal belonged to Constable Timothy McCutcheon."

McCutcheon, Morgan thought. Lizzie McCutcheon. At last . . . at long last, two pieces of the puzzle fit together.

"Where is McCutcheon?" Morgan asked. "I'd like to talk to him."

"Oh, I'm afraid that's quite impossible, Mr. Morgan."

"Look, I know these plainclothes agents have to keep low. I don't plan to expose him or anything. I just want to talk to him, to find out if he knows anything about this envelope."

"You don't understand," Bannister said. "It's not to protect his identity that you can't talk to him. You can't talk to him because he can't talk to anyone. You see, he's dead."

"Dead?" Suddenly Morgan remembered the news the constable in Juneau had told him . . . how four of their operatives had been killed in the last year.

"Yes, he was killed last spring while investigating the disappearance of . . ."

"Let me guess," Morgan interrupted. "He was investigating the disappearance of a shipment of guns, right?"

"Right you are, Mr. Morgan," Bannister said. "Now, I have answered all your questions. I believe you promised to tell me a story?" The constable refilled Morgan's cup and he held his hands around it, enjoying the warmth of the brew, even before he drank it.

"All right," Morgan said. He started then, beginning with the mysterious telegram that summoned him to Denver, and ending with the shootout on the trail in which he left four men dead and the remains of a shipment of guns scattered on the snow. He left out all the names, identifying them only as his "contacts."

"My," Bannister said. "That's the adventure stuff of a Beedle novel. And you say each of the brigands on the trail had one-hundred dollars in American money?"

"Yes," Morgan said. "At least, I think so. I found the money on the two who weren't blown apart by the dynamite, and I found another $120 lying scattered about on the snow. I'm sure the other two had a hundred apiece but it was destroyed by the blast."

"And one-hundred dollars American on Sourdough Mike," Bannister said. He stroked his chin. "Whoever is trying to kill you has certainly established the price."

"Yeah," Morgan said. He smiled. "But I'm gettin' expensive for the sonofabitch."

"Maybe that will be a break in our favor," Bannister suggested. "He may decide that he will have to pay a much larger sum to ensure that the job is done. If the sum is large enough, the news of the offer will have to get around."

"Yeah, could be," Morgan agreed, though he had no desire to wait around as bait while the offer increased. He remembered the man he was supposed to meet for Lizzie. "Do you know a fella named Big Ben Crowder?"

Bannister looked up sharply. "What about him?"

"Nothing," Morgan said. "I just wanted to know if you knew him, that's all."

"Yes, I know him. Funny you should ask. He was Timothy's stepfather. That's an interesting coincidence, don't you think?"

"Yeah, I guess it is."

"Of course, they never got along."

"Why not?"

"Mr. Crowder is what you might call an enterprising fellow. He is making a great deal of money out of the gold rush, yet he has never so much as picked up a nugget. We have a saying up here. Some folks get wealthy mining the hills, others make a fortune mining the men."

"And Crowder mines the men?"

"Yes."

"Is he dealing in guns?"

"Yes, as a matter of fact, he is. He has a license.

Of course, that was one of the things he and Timothy had difficulty over. Mr. Crowder thought that he should be given a license out of hand, just because he was Timothy's stepfather. Timothy, on the other hand, thought it smacked of corruption to have a relative—even an indirect relative such as a stepfather—get a license. I'm afraid Timothy fought against it . . . almost got it stopped."

"You don't think Crowder—"

"Had anything to do with young Timothy's death?" Bannister finished the question for him. He shook his head. "No, I don't think so. Of course, I did look into the matter. It was my duty, after all, and there had been that disagreement between them. Too, I have learned, Mr. Morgan, that despite the sudden eruption of gunfire between two armed and angry strangers, that the greatest number of homicides are committed by people who knew each other and, more often than not, are related. So, it wouldn't have been a great stretch of the imagination to believe that Ben Crowder could have killed Timothy. But my investigation convinced me that that wasn't the case."

"Where might I find Ben Crowder?"

"If I were looking for the gentleman, I should try the North Star Saloon," Bannister said.

"Thanks," Morgan said. He started toward the door then looked back. "By the way, does Ben Crowder have a middle name?"

"A middle name? No, not that I know of. Oh, wait, yes, I remember now, I did see a middle name when he applied for the license to handle the firearms. Just a moment, let me look it up." Bannister opened a file drawer and looked through several papers until he found what he was searching for. He pulled up a folder, opened it, then ran his finger down the page about halfway. He smiled. "Ah, yes, here it is."

"What is it?"

"Jacques," Bannister said. "Benjamine Jacques Crowder."

12

The North Star Saloon was a brightly lighted edifice with all the comforts of home. During the summer months riverboat traffic on the Yukon was so thick that some made the comment a person could walk from Dawson to Whitehorse without once getting his feet wet. That same river traffic brought all the necessities of life, plus many of the niceties. As a result, the North Star Saloon had a piano, a chandelier, and a huge, bevel edged mirror behind the bar.

The liquor was flowing freely and a piano player was grinding away a song as Morgan stepped into the place. He saw a table near the back wall and walked over to take it. A round faced man with a half-smoked cigar came to see what he wanted.

"Do you serve food in here?" Morgan asked, realizing that he had eaten nothing but jerky since the vennison steak he had with Lizzie several days ago.

"We got some caribou stew," the man said.

"All right, bring me some. And a beer."

The man turned away from the table but. Morgan called to him and he turned back.

"You know a fella name Big Ben Crowder?"

"What do you want with him?'

"I got a message from his stepdaughter," Morgan said.

"Yeah, I know 'im."

"Would you point him out to me?"

The man looked around, then shook his head. "He ain't in here."

Morgan grunted, then let the man go to take care of his order. A moment later he had the beer, and a few moments after that, a plate of something hot and steaming called stew by the man who put it on his table.

Morgan lifted a piece of the meat with his fork and tried to identify what else was in the stew but he had no luck. He raised some of it to his nose and sniffed.

"Hell, mister, if you ever et dog, you can sure as hell eat this."

Morgan looked up to see a man who had to be Big Ben Crowder. He remembered Lizzie's description, half polar bear, half Eskimo . . . or in this case, half Athabascan Indian. Morgan, like many of the new visitors, called all Alaskan and Northwest Territory natives Eskimos. In fact, he learned there were four major groups . . . Eskimos, who were around the northern and northwestern rim of Alaska, Alieuts who were out on the island chain, Tlingits, around the southern rim and coastal areas of British Columbia, and Athabascans in the interior.

"You'd be Big Ben Crowder," Morgan said.

"I heard you was lookin' for me," Crowder said. He pulled a chair away from the table, turned it around backwards, then sat on it, leaning on the back to look at Morgan. "You're the fella shot Sourdough Mike, aren't you?"

"Friend of yours?"

Crowder guffawed loudly. "Mister, Sourdough never had no friends. No family neither, I don't reckon. Folks say he was birthed by a caribou and suckled by a she-wolf. He was mean as they come an' they won't nobody be sheddin' no tears at his wake."

"That's good to hear. I wouldn't want anyone tryin' to get even for him."

"That ain't gonna happen. Some folks is liable to get a mite put out with you for not bringin' in the dynamite an' pistols like you was supposed to. Me included."

"How'd you know about that?" Morgan asked, his eyes narrowing in curiosity.

"Charley said you was lookin' for me, had a message from my stepdaughter. She had a shipment of dynamite an' guns she was sendin' up here. I figure you're the one she sent them by."

"That's right."

"But you lost 'em, right?"

"No," Morgan said. "I still got 'em."

"What? Where?"

"I cached 'em out on the trail a ways," he said. "I got jumped once, I figured I might get jumped again, so I hid 'em out."

"Mister, the word I got is they's blood an' shit lying all over the snow out there. I figured you blowed ever'thin' up when you was jumped."

"One case of dynamite, about four handguns," Morgan said. "I got everythin' else."

Crowder rubbed his chin and studied Morgan for a few moments. "Uh, huh," he said. "And what kind of handguns would them be?"

"What difference does it make?"

"None, I don't reckon," Crowder agreed. " 'Course, iffen they was Remingtons, I'd figure you was tellin' the truth an' you brung 'em in for my stepdaughter. But if they was Colts, I'd be figurin' you for Harrison Chapel's man, the self same man I'm supposed to be meetin'."

"Your stepdaughter said you wouldn't be particular about whether you bought from her or the Colt representative," Morgan said.

"My stepdaughter's a smart girl. She knows I ain't gonna let family get in the way of business." Crowder suddenly smiled. "I'll be damned," he said.

"What is it?"

"You got both of 'em, don't you? You're representin' Remington and Colt."

"What makes you say that?"

"I'm s'posed to meet a man here," Crowder said. "A man who's workin' for Harrison Chapel. Would you be that man?"

"I might be."

Crowder laughed. "Yes, sir, it's just like I said. You're representin' both companies. Now, how do you like that?"

"Since you've had so many questions for me, now I'll ask you a couple."

"Go right ahead."

"Who set up the ambush out on the trail? Who tried to have me killed?"

"Hell, that could be one of half a dozen men," Crowder said. "Anyone who wants the guns bad enough could do that."

"How did he know they were comin' in?"

"Ever'body knew they were comin' in. Lizzie hasn't exactly been keepin' it a secret. She was ready to sell to the highest bidder, no matter what that might be."

"I see. All right then, that explains why the ambush on the trail. I had the guns, somebody else wanted them. But why the ambush down at the livery stable?"

"That, I can't help you with," Crowder said. He took off his fur cap and rubbed the top of his head. "I have to confess, I don't understand that at all. Folks don't normally go to all the trouble to kill a man, 'lessen there's somethin' in it for them. I guess the question you got to ask yourself is, who wants you dead? An' why?"

"I don't know," Morgan said. "But I intend to find out."

Morgan saw someone standing at the far end of the bar. It was the same man he saw showing so much interest in Carter's horse when he came out of the bank. "Excuse me," he said abrubtly. He got up as if he was going out, then when he was next to the man at the bar, he suddenly stepped right up to him. His gun was out in a flash and he jabbed the barrel into the man's side. The whole thing was done so quickly and so smoothly, that no one else saw a thing. Not even the patrons standing closest to the man at the bar knew what was going on.

"Mister," Morgan hissed. "You and me's gonna take a little walk."

"What?" the man asked, gasping aloud. "What are you talking about?"

"You know what I'm talking about. And you know what this is in your side, don't you?" When the man didn't answer, Morgan shoved the barrel harder into his side, hard enough to make the man catch his breath. "Don't you?"

"I . . . I reckon I do," the man said.

"Move," Morgan said.

"Move where? Where are we going?"

"We're going to do a little horse trading," Morgan said.

At Morgan's insistence, and nudging, the man left a half-full glass of whiskey on the bar and walked out the door. The two of them tramped through the snow and dark down to the livery barn.

"Mister, I wish you'd tell me what the hell you're up to," he said.

"You'll find out soon enough. Push the door open and go inside."

The man opened the door and stepped into the livery barn. Morgan came in too, then closed the door behind him.

"You gonna tell me what this is all about?"

"No, mister, you're gonna tell me," Morgan said. "I want to know why you were so interested in the horse I rode in on."

"I told you, I was just admiring the animal. He's—"

That was as far as he got, because Morgan backhanded him. Surprised, the man took a couple of steps backward, then reached a hand up to his lips to feel the blood from the blow. "What'd you do that for?"

"I don't like bein' lied to," Morgan said. "And more important, I don't like bein' bushwhacked."

The man stared at Morgan sullenly.

"Empty your pockets," Morgan growled.

"Oh, I see. You're robbin' me, is that it? Well, I don't have much money but you're welcome to what I do have." He stuck his hand in one pocket and pulled out a roll of bills. "I've got a little over forty dollars."

"Turn 'em all out," Morgan said.

The man began emptying his pockets, making a little pile of his belongings on the flat top of a post. He had a pocket knife, a couple of keys, some change, and two little pieces of paper. Morgan recognized the papers, they were exactly like the paper he had been given by the bank when he converted Canadian money to American money. Morgan picked up one of them.

"Exchanged by the Dawson Canadian Security Bank," the receipt read. "Received from customer, $440 in Canadian currency . . . given to customer, $400 in American currency." The paper was dated two days earlier. Morgan put that one down and picked up another one. This one was dated today, and it exchanged $110 Canadian for $100 American.

"Well, now," Morgan said. "I find this very interesting. This is exactly the amount of money that's been paid to have me killed."

"That . . . that doesn't prove a thing," the man said.

Morgan's eyes grew flat and cold. "You're a dumb sonofabitch, aren't you?"

"What do you mean?"

Morgan raised his pistol and pointed it at the man's head.

"Mister, this isn't a court of law," Morgan said. "I don't need to prove you tried to kill me. All I have to do is believe it. I'm the judge and the jury. I believe you did it, and I'm going to kill you."

"No! No, wait!" the man said, raising his hands and crossing them before his face, as if by that action he could stop the bullet. "Don't shoot me, please, for God's sake, don't shoot me. I'll talk . . . I'll tell you everything."

"What do you mean you'll tell me everything? I already know you're the one who paid the money to have me ambushed. What the hell else do I need to know?" He cocked it.

"No!" the man screamed. "I was workin' for someone else! If you kill me, you still won't know who's after you!"

It was what Morgan wanted to hear, and the reason he had taken such a drastic step in the first place. He had no real intention of killing the man, but the man didn't know that. Morgan hesitated for a moment, pretending that he was thinking about it.

"Hell, mister, don't you understand? They's someone tryin' to get total control of all the guns that come into Alaska and the Territories." He laughed, a terrified, insane cackle. "You think those few guns and dynamite you was carryin' was the only loot in this whole deal? Mister, they's millions in this. Millions! Whoever winds up controllin' all the weapons controls everything."

"Are you telling me one of the legitimate gun manufacturers, Remington, or Colt, or somebody like that is behind this?" Morgan asked.

"Shit . . . they don't know nothin'," the man said. "What do they know? All they know is how to make the guns. They don't have any idea what's goin' on up here. The only one that did suspect somethin' was Tim McCutcheon, and he got hisself kilt soon as he started pokin' aroun'. Same as you . . . only you didn't get kilt."

"Right," Morgan said. "I didn't get killed. But someone is trying awfully hard, and mister, if you don't tell me in one second who it is—"

That was as far as Morgan got before the lights went out. He felt a crushing blow to the top of his head, and he went down like a sack of flour.

13

Like a cork surfacing from far beneath the surface of the water, Lee Morgan slowly floated back to consciousness. When he opened his eyes he saw that he was lying in a bed, well covered and warm. A kerosene lantern burned on the bedside table, the wick turned down so that the flame was a subdued glow rather than a bright glare.

Morgan tried to sit up but a sharp pain on the top of his head and a quick nausea made him lie back down. He turned his head from side to side to try and figure out where he was. There was nothing in the room to give him a clue, though he was fairly sure it wasn't a hotel room.

The door opened and someone came into the room carrying a tray. There was a steaming bowl of broth on the tray and even in his condition, Morgan appreciated the aroma, remembering that he had not finished his stew earlier. Today? Yesterday? When? This accursed constant darkness was enough to drive a man crazy when it came around to trying to figure time.

The woman carrying the tray was a large boned, round faced, Indian woman. She set the tray down on a table next to the bed.

"I have to admit that looks good," Morgan said.

The woman didn't respond, either by word or expression.

"Where am I?" Morgan asked.

The woman started to leave.

"Hey, wait a minute!" Morgan called to her. "Who are you? What is this place? Where the hell am I?"

The door was suddenly blocked out by a gaint of a man and for a moment Morgan thought it was Big Ben Crowder. Then, as the man stepped through the door, Morgan saw that it wasn't Crowder, it was Chotauk.

"Chotauk!" Morgan said. In his surpise he tried to sit up, but again the pain pushed him back down. "What the hell are you doing up here?" he asked.

"This my home," Chotauk said. "Woman who feed you is my wife."

"Well I'll be damned," Morgan said. Moving more slowly, he was finally able to sit up. There was a crust of hot bread near the broth and he broke a piece of it off and popped it in his mouth. He didn't think he had ever tasted anything more delicious.

"Miss Chapel think you were dead," Chotauk said.

"Yeah," Morgan said, rubbing the top of his head gingerly. "Well, for a while there I thought so too."

"No, not this bump on head," Chotauk said. "Before. Men come, say fishermen find your body."

"Yeah, well Chapel said he would explain all that to his niece," Morgan said. "That was his idea, not mine. Wait a minute . . . you mean he didn't tell her?"

"No," Mariellen said, coming into the room at that moment. "The only word I got was that you were dead."

"Damn," Morgan said. He started to reach for the broth, but Mariellen came over and sat on the bed beside him.

"Let me do that," she said, picking up the bowl and spooning some into Morgan's mouth.

"Been a long time since anyone did this," Morgan said.

"Your mother?"

"No. Some girl down in Abiline," Morgan teased.

"Uh huh, maybe you'd like me to spill this on your lap."

"No, no," Morgan said, laughing gently.

He noticed that Chotauk had withdrawn. Mariellen spooned another bite into his mouth and he took it and studied her for a long moment. There had been the girl down in Denver . . . the one who was going to poison him, then the girl in Juneau, and Lizzie McCutcheon. But Morgan realized now, probably for the first time, that every one of them had just been substitutes. Mariellen was the one he wanted, and had wanted since he first met her down in Denver more than two months ago.

"I'm glad," Mariellen finally said.

"Glad?"

"That you aren't dead."

"Why, thank you, Miz Mariellen," Morgan said.

"You don't need to do that here."

"That's good."

Mariellen gave him another spoonful.

"What are you doing up here?"

"Chotauk and I brought in a load of handguns this morning."

"Where did you get them? The shipment Chotauk and I picked up at Juneau was nothing but rocks."

"Oh, didn't I tell you? I had another shipment ordered besides that one," Mariellen said. "It came in three days later without a hitch."

"Your uncle didn't tell me anything about that shipment."

"My uncle didn't know," Mariellen said. "We had a disagreement about how to get the guns up here. I wanted to show him my way would work so I tried it."

"And it worked?"

"Yes."

Morgan chuckled. "I'll bet you're the talk of the town right now," he said. "Everyone's been trying to get a load in and you're the only one to succeed."

"Oh, no one knows they're here yet," Mariellen said. "Chotauk hid them."

"What about Skagway Annie?" Morgan said. "Didn't she get a little curious about where you were going?"

Mariellen laughed. "Poor Skagway Annie. I'm afraid I wasn't very nice to her when I thought she was responsible for your disappearance. There was a fire . . . terrible thing, actually, it destroyed her hotel, saloon, why, would you believe that the flames even leaped two blocks away, sparing everything else but landing on a laundry she happened to own?"

"Sounds like a pretty educated fire to me," Morgan said.

"Yes, wasn't it? Tell me, Mr. Lee Morgan. How is it we found you lying on the snow in the livery with your head cracked open? Who hit you?"

"I don't know," Morgan answered. "Was there anyone else there? A thin, hooknosed, beady eyed man with a scraggly beard?"

"Should there have been?"

"I was talkin' to him when I got hit," Morgan said. "He's the one that's been trying to have me killed ever since I got here. He was just about to tell me who was paying him when the lights went out. There are a whole lot of things that just don't add up, Mariellen, but I figure that man has the answers."

"Yeah, well, you're going to have to find them somewhere else."

"Somewhere else? Why? What do you mean?"

"They found someone fitting that description down by the river," Mariellen said.

"Dead?"

"Shot right between the eyes."

"Damn."

"His name was Billy Joe Collins," Mariellen said. "That mean anything to you?"

"No, not really, I never . . . wait a minute. What did you say his name was?"

"Billy Joe Collins."

"B.J.C."

"Is that supposed to mean something?"

"Well, I don't know. I thought I had that part worked out. Now I'm not so sure."

Mariellen laughed. "Mr. Morgan, would it be possible that your brains are all scrambled up, like a mess of pork brains and eggs?"

"I don't know, maybe it doesn't make any sense," he said. He waved away another bite. "I've had enough."

Mariellen put the bowl down, then looked at him with eyes that were smoldering. "It's about time," she said. "I've got another treatment in mind now, and it has nothing to do with food."

"Oh? What sort of treatment would that be?" Morgan asked.

Mariellen began unbuttoning the fastenings on her heavy wool shirt. "It's a little hard to explain," she said. "I'm going to have to show you."

Morgan lay back on the pillow and watched as Mariellen removed her shirt, then the undershirt beneath it, then her undergarments.

Morgan wasn't a poetic man, he was not one to put into words things he felt, but he did have a sense of appreciation for things in a way that some men would say were poetic. He liked the sight of a lone candle in a window on a dark night . . . the sound of a swiftly moving stream of water . . . clouds when they were underlit by the setting sun . . . flowers in the wild. These were things that were special to him, though he could never say so. But if he ever did get around to making a compilation of what made life sweet, he would have to add to the list what he was seeing right now. Mariellen Chapel, her skin pink and glowing, her nipples drawn tight by the cold, the hair at the junction of her legs shadowed in mystery, was standing before him in all her nude glory.

Morgan had seen his share of naked women, some beautiful, some functional, and some whose nudity gave meaning to the word obscene. He may have even seen women more beautiful than Mariellen, but in the sum total of things, in this place and in this time, no one in the world could have made a more pleasurable impact on his senses than this girl did.

"Aren't you going to take off your shirt?" Mariellen asked.

"I intend to take off more than my shirt," Morgan said.

Mariellen laughed, a low, throaty laugh. "I don't think so," she said.

"Oh? Why not?"

"You don't have anything but a shirt on," Mariellen said.

Even as she spoke, Morgan felt his erection rubbing against the sheet. He realized now that it had been growing, unrestrained, from the moment she started stripping for him. It was just that he had been so appreciative of what he was seeing that he didn't realize it.

"Let me take it off for you," Mariellen said, and she leaned over to grasp the shoulders of the shirt in her hands.

As she did so her breasts swung forward and the nipple of one of them brushed against Morgan's lips. He opened his mouth and took her nipple inside, sucking on it, running his tongue over the congested little nub. She moaned in pleasure, and leaned into him for just a moment, the she pulled the shirt over his head and tossed it aside.

Morgan's penis was as hard and as rigid as stone. Already so engorged with blood as to be petrified, it was ready to perform whatever task he asked of it, to give no quarter until the sensations that had turned it to stone waned, allowing it to return to flesh again. Mariellen went to him, flushed and panting. She was trembling in every limb and her eyes were awash with tears of excitement. She pulled the covers back exposing Morgan, looking down at the organ which stood like a raised arm.

Without a word, Mariellen lowered to her knees, opened her mouth, closed it over his penis, and slid it a good way down her throat. Morgan brought his hands up to rest lightly on her soft hair. She moaned, then moved on down until her lips surrounded the very root of his member. Morgan looked down at her. Her eyes were half closed and fluttering, her cheeks deeply dimpled from the suction she was beginning to apply. Then she lifted one hand and gingerly cupped his balls, lolling her tongue around with the instinctive skill of a hungry calf. Morgan reached down and, with thumb and forefinger, teasingly pinched and pulled at her nipples. Through her left breast he could feel the wild pounding of her heart.

With a talent born of her desire, she sucked and lolled his penis, at the same time massaging his scrotum, moving along his member with varying pressures from base to tip, then swiftly reabsorbing him to its hairy hilt. Morgan could feel a familiar sensation deep in his loins, a sensation which grew stronger with her every movement and touch.

Then, exerting a little pressure on her head with his hands, he stopped her, and with a tortured sigh, she rose to her feet. "Don't you like?" she asked.

"Yeah," Morgan grunted. "But I wouldn't want to spoil our fun by finishing too fast."

Mariellen smiled at him and then threw a leg over his chest, mounting him as if she were mounting a horse. "Well, then," she said. "Maybe you can do it to me for a little while now."

Morgan waited expectantly as she moved the swollen, foam flecked lips of her sex to his mouth. With his first good taste of her he felt a frenzy of excitement, reaming her with his tongue as she quivered against it and squeezed it until the very roots hurt. Finally she pulled away from him.

"I want you in me now," she said. "I want to feel it deep inside."

Morgan rolled her over, noticing almost as an aside that his head no longer hurt . . . that he felt no more nausea from his movement. He thrust himself in her, shoving it up and in, hammering against the furthermost membrane of her being. She gnashed her teeth and rolled her eyes until only the whites showed and contorted against him as she was ravaged by her climax. Then, when she was in the middle of her orgasmic throes, he ejaculated, sending vast quantities of semen gushing into her to comingle with her own juices, then to drip out onto the bedsheet beneath them.

When he awakened later, she was sleeping curled up next to him, her head nestled against his shoulder, her leg thrown over his, her hand curled possessively around his flaccid member. It was dark, but that didn't mean a thing in this damned country. It could have been three o'clock in the morning, or three o'clock in the afternoon. It didn't matter. For the moment, the rest of the world could go to hell.

This was nice. This was really nice.

14

"Lee? Lee, are you awake?"

Morgan opened his eyes and realized that he was still in bed. Mariellen was standing just inside the door of the bedroom, as fully dressed as if she were going to church. For a moment he had to force himself to realize that the woman he was looking at now was the same woman who had been so much a part of his primordal urges a little earlier.

"Uh, yes," he said. "Yes, I'm awake."

"There is someone in the parlor to see you," Mariellen said. "Do you feel up to it?"

Morgan sat up. The pain was gone and only a small amount of the dizziness remained. He swung his legs over, realizing as he did so that he was still nude.

"I'll, uh, wait in the hall," Mariellen said quickly, and Morgan noticed that she actually blushed. He smiled at that. How could she still blush after everything they had done together, and for each other?

A few moments later, Morgan stepped out into

the hall, fully dressed. Mariellen was waiting for him.

"Who is it?" Morgan asked.

"An old acquaintance of yours, I believe," Mariellen said.

Morgan followed Mariellen to the parlor of Chotauk's house. There, he saw Big Ben Crowder waiting for him.

"So," Ben said, smiling and extending his hand. "I learn that the man who called himself Hank Leslie is actually Lee Morgan?"

"Yes," Morgan admitted.

"And you are a representative for Colt Firearms?"

"Yes," Morgan said again.

Crowder laughed. "So much for my stepdaughter's innocent faith in you," he said.

"Crowder, I never told your stepdaughter I wasn't working for Colt Firearms. And I planned to make good on that delivery for her too. I was bushwhacked, if you remember."

"Ah, yes, I do remember."

"Anyway, you knew I was working for Colt Firearms. You did have instructions to meet me, didn't you? Aren't you B.J.C.?"

"Yes," Crowder said. "I'm sorry about the initials, but when I realized that Billy Joe Collins and I had the same initials, I thought I might be able to use that. Unfortunately he's dead now, so he'll be of no further use to me."

"Who killed him?"

"Yes, yes, that's very good," Crowder said. "Keep sayin' it just that way."

"Keep sayin' what?"

"Why, that you had nothin' to do with killin' Billy Joe Collins, of course."

"I didn't kill him."

"Morgan, this is Big Ben Crowder you're talkin' to, remember. We were sittin' together when you suddenly left the table and went up to Billy Joe at the bar. A moment later you walked out with him. I was just naturally curious, so I followed you to the livery."

"All right, you followed me. So what?"

"I heard a shot 'bout halfway there, so I commenced to run the rest of the distance. When I come up on the two of you, you was lyin' there with your gun in your hand an' Billy Joe was just across from you with a bullet hole 'twixt his eyes an' a zap in his hand."

"A what?"

"A zap. That's a little sack made out of hide, filled with lead balls. A good rap on the head can do a man in. Lucky for you, Billy Joe didn't kill you."

"Goddamnit, Crowder, Billy Joe didn't hit me. He didn't hit me, an' I didn't shoot him."

"I'm only tellin' what I seen an' done," Crowder said. "Anyhow, I seen the two of you lyin' there, him dead, you purt' near that way, so I done what I figured should be done. I got a'holt of Billy Joe's body an' I carried 'im outta the livery an' dumped him down by the river. That way, when you was found, folks thought someone just come up on you an' give you a good rap on the head."

"That is what happened, and I'm tired of you makin' more of it."

Crowder held out his hands. "Look, you don't have to convince me o'nothin'. I ain't the law. 'Sides which, I'm in this here thing as deep as you are now. I'm the one carted the body away, remember? An' I also put a bullet back in your gun so's no one could tell you'd just fired it."

"Goddamnit,I didn't fire it."

"Maybe not, maybe somebody else did an' put it in your hand," Crowder said. "Anyhow, I told Constable Bannister that I seen someone runnin' away from the livery. 'Course, that was when he was tryin' to find out who hit you . . . he didn't know nothin' 'bout Billy Joe then. That didn't come 'till later when someone found his body right where I put it."

Morgan shook his head, then he thought of something. "Tell me, Crowder, what about the liveryman? Where was he all this time?"

"Did you see him?"

"No."

"I didn't either. Fac' is, I hear tell the constable is lookin' for him, but he ain't found him neither."

"He's the key to all this," Morgan said. "If we could find him, he could tell us what happened . . . who it was that hit me from the rear."

"Yes, well, I don't reckon it matters none now," Crowder said. "I took what money Billy Joe had, so the constable thinks he was murdered an' robbed. He ain't put the two of you together at all. We can jus' let that drop an' get on to other business."

"What sort of business?"

Crowder smiled broadly. "Why, gun business, of course," he said. He looked over at Mariellen who had been present for the entire conversation, but had said nothing. "You have told him about the guns, ain't you?"

"He knows that Chotauk and I brought up a load, yes," she answered.

Crowder chuckled. "Ain't that somethin'? A

woman bringin' in guns like that, after so many others have failed? We been waitin' six months for a shipment of guns, and here this little ole' gal brings up a load." Crowder rubbed his hands together as if anticipating a feast. "Tell me, Miss Mariellen, how many guns did you bring?"

"One hundred and fifty."

"A hunnert an' fifty? What kind? Was they all handguns?"

"Peacemakers, every one of them," Mariellen said.

"Good, good. Them's the best kind," Crowder said. He leaned back in his chair and crossed his arms across his chest. "You hear that?" he asked Morgan. "Peacemakers."

"I heard."

"This here is your lucky day, Miss Mariellen," Crowder went on. "I'm gonna give you one-hundred dollars apiece for each an' ever' one of them guns."

Mariellen didn't say a word.

"Didn't you hear me?" Crowder asked, smiling broadly. "A hunnert dollars apiece. That's fifteen thousand dollars."

"Yes, I can do my math," Mariellen said.

"Well, I was beginnin' to wonder if you heard me there. I guess you was just took back over how much money you just made yourself. Yes, sir, let these here fools break rocks for their gold. This is a much better way, don't you think?" Crowder stood up. "When will you be bringin' the guns to me?"

"I haven't said I'll do it, yet," Mariellen said.

The smile froze on Crowder's face. "What do you mean?"

"I thought the meaning was quite clear, Mr.

Crowder. I haven't accepted your offer."

"Why the hell not?" Crowder exploded. "You ain't plannin' on gettin' no better offer from anyone, are you?"

"I don't know. I suppose that's a possibility. I would like to wait and see."

Crowder got up from the chair and walked over to the halltree where he recovered his parka. He started putting it on. His eyes narrowed as he looked over at Mariellen.

"It was my thinkin', Miss Chapel, that we, meanin' me an' you, an' your uncle, had us a understandin' about all this. We was gonna stake out a marketplace for the Colt Firearm Company."

He looked over at Morgan. "Hell, you're supposed to be a representative for Colt Firearms. What do you say to all this?"

"You're telling us this is all out of loyalty to Colt?" Morgan asked.

"You're damn right it is. When Big Ben Crowder makes a business deal, he sticks to it. I said I would sell Colts in the Klondike, and I will."

"If that's the case, Crowder, why were you so willin' to take the shipment of Remingtons from me?" Morgan asked.

"You know why I was takin' 'em. My stepdaughter was tryin' to make a few dollars an' I was willin' to help out, that's all. 'Sides which, I figured to buy 'em and take 'em off the market."

"Yeah," Morgan said. "Well, you weren't the only one wantin' to take 'em off the market. That's why Billy Joe Collins sent the welcomin' party out to meet me."

Crowder had his parka and fur hat on now, and

he looked at Morgan in puzzlement when Morgan said that about the welcoming party.

"Look here, are you tellin' me that Billy Joe was the one tried to have you ambushed?"

"That's right."

"I'll be damned. I never figured him for much more'n a cheap crook. Didn't figure he had enough sense to get involved in anythin' this big."

"He wasn't in it alone," Morgan said. "That's what I was talkin' to him about. He was about ready to tell me who was backing him, when I got hit over the head."

Crowder stroked his chin for a moment. "All right, maybe you didn't kill him," he conceded. "All I know is what I found an' to me it looked bad . . . so bad that I figured I ought to change it before someone else seen it. If I done wrong, I'm sorry . . . but I was just tryin' to do you a favor."

"Yeah, well, I hope that favor don't come back to haunt me," Morgan said.

Crowder started toward the door, then looked over at Mariellen again.

"Miss Chapel, I think you're gonna find that there's plenty of money to be made up here, iffen we don't none of us get too greedy. What we've got to do is all of us got to work together . . . just like me an' your uncle has done . . . and just like I done for you, Morgan, when I carried off Billy Joe's body. I hope the two of you think some about what I'm telling you. I'll see you around."

"I'll be damned," Morgan said, after Crowder left.

"What?"

"He didn't make me an offer for the guns he

thinks I've got hid out."

"Do you have some guns hidden on the trail?" Mariellen asked.

"No, but he doesn't know that. Just before I had my run-in with whoever knocked me out, I told Crowder that I had off-loaded some of the guns before the ambush. He was so anxious to get the guns from you, why didn't he make me an offer?"

"I don't know," Mariellen said. "You just told him you had guns hidden, but you didn't really, is that right?"

"Right."

Mariellen laughed. "That's funny," she said. "That's really funny."

"Why is it so funny?"

"I don't have any guns either."

"Would you mind tellin' me why the hell you're letting it be known that you have guns if you don't?"

"Simple," Mariellen said. "If you want to catch whose been raiding your hen house, you set out a chicken. I'm just dangling a little bait, that's all."

"You were part of the bait," Morgan said.

"I suppose I was."

"If you've spent any time around traps, Mariellen, you notice that even when you catch what you're after, the bait nearly always gets eaten. You were taking an awful risk."

"I had Chotauk with me."

"One of the men who came after me on the trail had a .50 Sharps," Morgan growled. "A .50 Sharps will drop a buffalo, a polar bear, a grizzly, and, Miss Mariellen, it will drop Chotauk."

"What about you?" Mariellen asked. "You did

the same thing, didn't you?"

"That's different."

"Why? Because you're a man and I'm a woman?"

"That might have something to do with it," Morgan agreed.

"Lee Morgan, they call me the Queen of the Klondike for a very good reason," Mariellen said. "I run this country up here, and I run it because I know how, and when to take chances. I'm not some little schoolmarm from Denver, I'm an arctic she-wolf. And I remind you that a bullet will go through you just as easily as it will through me. So don't tell me how to run my business."

Morgan laughed and held up his hands in mock surrender. "All right, all right," he said. "But, if we're both going after the same critters, with the same bait, then the least we can do is work together."

Mariellen smiled sweetly. "Now, Lee Morgan, you are making sense. You'll find I'm a lot easier to get along with when you're working with me, instead of against me."

15

"I must say, you and your lady friend have created quite a furor in town," Constable Bannister said as he poured a cup of steaming tea, first for Morgan, then for himself.

"Yeah," Morgan replied. "I never knew that many people were gun fanciers."

Bannister laughed. "Gun fanciers, oh that's good," he said. "Yes, that is good indeed." He blew on the surface of his tea then slurped it over the rim of his cup. "You are both in quite a bit of danger, you know," he added.

"I suppose so," Morgan agreed.

"Tell me, Mr. Morgan, why do I get the distinct impression that this is exactly what you wanted?"

"Constable, there have already been several good men killed while trying to open up the market for handguns. I don't think they were just isolated cases. I think there is a grand design behind it all."

"To what end, Mr. Morgan?"

"Do you know how much money a single

handgun can bring in this town?"

"Yes, I do. I was quite astounded to hear that people are willing to pay up to $150 for a pistol."

"That's a lot of money," Morgan said. "You could sell two thousand pistols here in Dawson, at least that many in Whitehorse, and in all of the Territorites and Alaska, probably as many as twenty-thousand handguns. Are you adding all that up?"

Bannister let out a low whistle. "That's three million dollars," he noted.

"Yes, and it's a hell of a lot easier than blasting holes in the sides of mountains or panning an icy stream."

"And you believe there is someone behind all this, trying to corner the market?"

"Yes."

"You may very well be right, Mr. Morgan." Bannister got up from his chair and walked over to a file drawer. He opened it, then looked through the papers until he pulled out a large, brown envelope. He brought the envelope over to Morgan.

"What's that?"

"This, Mr. Morgan, is something that I could get into trouble over, if it were known that I shared it with you. It's the last report submitted by Timothy McCutcheon."

Morgan opened the envelope and took out the single page report. It had been composed on a typewriting machine and was very easy to read.

REPORT ON UNSOLVED MURDERS
IN TERRITORIES AND ALASKA
SUBMITTED BY
FIELD AGENT TIMOTHY McCUTCHEON

1. In the last year there have been five (5) unsolved murders in portions of the Northwest Territories and U.S. Alaska.

2. The method in which each of these men were killed, and the events leading up to the discovery of their bodies, have differed in every case. Two of the victims were long time residents of the north country, three were newcomers.

3. There has been one thing common to all five murders. Each of the victims were engaged in gun dealing, either in the introduction of weapons into the territories, or the distribution of guns already available.

4. It is the conclusion of this agent that the murders are not random, but rather the design of a person or persons who, for their own nefarious scheme, wishes to eliminate all who deal in firearms.

5. My personal investigation has led me to believe that Mr. Frank Church, a local businessman, should be questioned about his possible involvement in this.

Morgan put the report back into the envelope, then looked up at Bannister. "What did headquarters say about this report?"

"Nothing," Bannister said.

"Nothing? Why not?"

"They never received the report."

"Why not?"

Bannister pointed to the envelope. "You'll

notice that the report was done on a typewriting machine?"

"Yes."

"And it wasn't sighed," Bannister went on. "Without McCutcheon's handwritten report, or, at the very least, his signature affixed thereto, this isn't a valid report. As it was done on one of those machines, it could have been prepared by anyone . . . for any reason. Therefore, officially, the report doesn't even exist."

"What about unofficially?"

"Unofficially, I tried to submit it," Bannister said. "I sent it under the cover of my own letter, handwritten and signed, by me, attesting to the authenticity of the document. But regulations are regulations, Mr. Morgan, and I'm afraid it was to no avail. The document came back to me with a note saying that it would not be received."

"But you said it would get you in trouble if you showed it to anyone."

"Yes, even though it is not a valid document, it is still the official property of the Northwest Mounted Police, and therefore not authorized to be viewed by any civilian."

"What about this man, Frank Church? Have you spoken with him?"

"I've tried . . . believe me, I've tried. He has an office in a small room above the mercantile store, but he hasn't been seen there for several months now."

"Any idea where he is?"

"He left word that he was going to spend the winter in the States. He asked the mercantile store to hold his mail for him."

"Did you take a look at his mail?"

Bannister smiled. "I did," he said. "I had no

authority to do so, but I feel that sometimes investigations, if they are to bear fruit, need not necessarily be restrained by lines of authorization. Therefore, I managed to take a look at the mail once, when the proprietor of the mercantile store wasn't looking."

"What did you find?"

"Nothing of any help, I'm afraid. A few responses from mail order houses, a calendar from a Denver bank, and a bill for some engraved stationery. No personal letters, nothing to give a clue as to where he might be, or when he might be coming back."

"I wish I knew what made McCutcheon suspect him," Morgan said. He looked down at the report again, and noticed crease lines across the paper where it had once been folded. Curious, he refolded it, then reached in his pocket and removed the envelope he had been carrying ever since it was slipped under the door on board the ship coming up. The envelope too, had been folded over once, and the crease line in McCutcheon's report fit exactly with the crease line in the envelope.

"My word," Bannister said when he saw what Morgan had done. "It would appear that the report was once in that same envelope."

"Yes," Morgan said. He rubbed his chin as he looked at the envelope, now with the report inside. He tapped it with his finger. "Are you a betting man, Constable?"

"No, not really."

"Too bad, because I would be willing to bet a ton that this is the way the envelope was meant to reach me. But somehow, someone got to it before I did and they removed the report."

"But . . . how could that be?" Bannister asked. "The report is right here and has been all along."

"Go over to your file drawer and pull out three other reports," Morgan said. "No, pull out five."

Bannister looked puzzled. "Reports about what?"

"About anything, Constable," Morgan said. "It doesn't make any difference."

Shaking his head in confusion, the constable did as Morgan requested. He pulled out five reports and dropped the big, brown envelopes on the desk in front of Morgan.

"Open the envelopes and pull them out." Morgan suggested.

Bannister did so, then looked up at Morgan, still as confused as before.

"What do you see?" Morgan asked.

"Well, this report is asking for an increase in the allotment for food for the dog teams . . . this one deals with illegal gambling on the riverboats during the summer months . . . this one—"

"No," Morgan interrupted. "Don't look at what's on them, just look at them. What do you see?"

The confusion stayed on Bannister's face for a moment longer, then he suddenly smiled as he realized what Morgan was getting at. He pointed at them.

"They are all flat," he said. "Not one of them has been folded."

"Right. I realized as soon as I saw the large envelopes that it was so the reports wouldn't be folded. And yet this one was. Someone got in here, took the report out, folded it, and put it in this smaller envelope."

"Then that same person, or another person, took the report out of the small envelope and returned it to the large one," Bannister concluded.

"It looks that way," Morgan said. "Who else, besides you, can get into the files?"

"No one besides me, Mr. Morgan," Bannister said.

"Someone sure as hell did."

"Perhaps it was the person who gave you a whack," Bannister suggested.

Involuntarily, Morgan rubbed the top of his head. "I sure wish I knew who that was."

"Yes, well, the only witness we have is Mr. Crowder who found you lying on the ground and saw someone running out the back. Of course, the liveryman could substantiate that if I could just talk to him, but so far I haven't been able to do that," Bannister said. "I was hoping he might be able to tell us something, even if it was just to give me a list of people he saw at the stable that day."

"You still haven't found him?"

"No," Bannister said. "To tell you the truth, I'm beginning to suspect foul play. He hasn't been seen by anyone in four days."

"Has he ever left his stable that long before?"

"Oh, yes, frequently, when he goes to Whitehorse or someplace like that. But always before he has made some arrangement for his business. This time, he didn't appear to do that."

"Maybe he did see who whacked me over the head," Morgan said. "Although I don't remember seeing the liveryman around."

"Yes, and then there is the case of Billy Joe Collins," Bannister said. "I have to tell you, Mr. Morgan, had you not been found unconscious in the stable, you would have been my prime suspect in that case. You were seen leaving the

North Star with him."

"He had some information I wanted," Morgan said. "I was talking to him when someone hit me."

Bannister's eyes widened. "You were? See here, I wasn't aware of that."

"Were you aware that Billy Joe Collins is the man who paid to have me bushwhacked on the trail?"

"No."

"And were you also aware that he was the one who posed as a mounted policeman to pay the fella to try and shoot me at the livery stable the day I arrived?"

"No, I didn't know that either. Mr. Morgan, I hope you realize that the more you tell me now, the more you are piling suspicion upon yourself for his death."

"Yeah, but we come back to the same thing, don't we? I was lying unconscious on the ground in the livery, he was found dead down by the river. I sure didn't kill him there, then come back and hit myself over the head."

"Unless you killed him by the river, then came to the livery bent on taking your horse out to make good your escape, at which time you were attacked."

"Do you believe that's what happened?" Morgan asked. "Do you think I killed Collins?"

Bannister studied Morgan for a long moment, then shook his head slowly. "No, Mr. Morgan. I don't think you did. But I'll tell you what I'm afraid of."

"What?"

"We're going to find the liveryman just the way we did Mr. Collins. Belly up in the snow."

16

Clayton Summers urged the dogs on. There was a storm coming and he wanted to make as much time as he could before he was forced to stop. He'd heard there were Indian villages spread out all along the trail . . . no more than fifty miles apart, people said. He wouldn't know about that. He had never come this way before, nor had he ever traveled by dogsled. He had always come and gone by boat, leaving Dawson only in the summer months when travel was relatively easy.

He'd ventured up from Kansas a few years ago, intending to stay four years. His plan was to return home with enough money to buy a farm. He didn't quite have four years in Dawson yet, he had six months to go, but recent events made it seem like a good idea for him to leave while the leaving was good.

He thought back to what had happened four days ago. He had been lying in one of the stalls, wrapped in blankets and skins, keeping warm with a bottle of whiskey, when he heard Morgan and Collins come into the livery. He raised up when he heard Morgan threaten to shoot Collins. What happened next, happened so fast that Summers was taken totally by surprise. A man suddenly came out of nowhere to bash Morgan over the head. The man had his back to Summers, and he was dressed in furs so that it was impossible to tell who it was.

"Am I glad to see you," Collins had said.

"Don't be," the man replied.

That was when Summers saw the flash from the pistol, saw the black hole appear between Collins' eyes, then saw him go down. He got up then, and ran toward the back of the barn.

"Hey, you! Come back here!" the killer had shouted, as if Summers was crazy enough to actually do it.

Summers hadn't kept his money in the bank. It was a foreign bank and he didn't trust foreigners, so it was easy enough for him to go to his cache and take out the money he had saved. It was a little more difficult for him to get a dog team and sled together to leave. He had to pay twice what they were worth, and as dogs were the only means of transportion in and out of Dawson for several months at a time, they were worth a great deal.

Summers hated the damned dogs. Give him a horse anytime. The problem with a horse, of course, was that there was no way he could carry enough food for the animal. He had heard stories of horses dropping dead on the trail from starvation. Dogs would eat frozen salmon, that made them manageable, but as far as Summers was concerned, it sure as hell didn't make them any more desirable.

Summers urged the dogs on to greater and greater speed. He wanted to get away, to get all the way down to Juneau of possible. There, he would take the next boat south. He wondered how far he had to go, and he looked around to try and get his bearings.

Where the hell was he?

He had purposedly avoided the main trail because he was afraid that the killer would come after him, and since Summers was inexperienced with dog teams, the killer would have no difficulty in overtaking him. But since he left the trail, he was having more and more difficulty with navigation. He tried using the stars, but the sky had been so overcast for the last several hours that he had been unable to take a sighting. And now it was beginning to snow. The situation was getting much worse.

Manquit was on the route from a remote Athabascan village to Dawson early the next day, as soon as the storm had passed. He was a young, powerfully muscled Athabascan Indian, but even Manquit, who was used to such conditions, found it hard going on this steep, and little used trail. Then, as he topped one particularly steep rise, he came upon a pitiful sight.

A man, frozen stiff, his face blanketed with snow, huddled on the ground alongside a pitiful heap of frozen sled dogs. Manquit didn't know the name of the frozen white man, but he did recognize him as the one who ran the livery stable in Dawson. Using his knife and hatchet, Manquit managed to break the frozen body loose from the ice and load him into the sled for the journey back to Dawson.

The mysterious death of Clayton Summers was the talk of the North Star Saloon. At every table his name was mentioned, stories were told about him, and speculations were advanced as to why he would have taken his entire poke and just skedaddled in the middle of the winter like that. The fact that he was off the main route added fuel to the speculation, though many said that was just a result of his inexperience with dog teams. A few pointed out that the murder of Billy Joe Collins was still unsolved, and wondered if there was any connection between the two. Even Morgan's name was mentioned as he had been found unconscious in Summer's livery, and no one could recall having seen Summer since that time.

Morgan heard his name on a few lips as he went into the saloon, but he made no effort to hear what was being said or who was talking about him. He knew that he was the center of attention right now and, for his purposes, it didn't bother him. If he was right in the middle of things, he would better be able to see what was going on around him. He stepped up to the bar and ordered a whiskey.

The bartender poured him a drink, then moved down the bar to attend to another customer. Morgan turned his back to the bar and looked out over the room. There were two stoves roaring in the middle of the room and though they turned back the sub-zero weather, it could hardly be said that the saloon was comfortably warm. In fact, everyone here continued to wear their parkas and caps, though the heavy mittens were removed to facilitate drinking and handling of cards. Or guns, Morgan thought, though as he looked around he noticed that not too many men were actually carrying pistols, evidence of the need for the product he was representing.

Ensconced at his regular table across the room

near the wall was Big Ben Crowder. When Morgan looked toward him, Crowder invited him over. Morgan took his drink with him and crossed the room to join the big man.

"Well," Crowder said. "I'm sure that by now you and Miss Chapel have talked to each other and she knows that you've also got some handguns up here."

"We've talked," Morgan said.

"I figured you would," Crowder said. "I didn't bring it up in front of her 'cause she seemed to be tendin' to you pretty well an' if she knew you was in competition with her she might not be so friendly to you."

"It's good to know you were just lookin' out for my interests," Morgan said dryly.

"Yeah, I know, you don't believe me," Crowder said, "but it is true. Now I think it's time you an' me come to some sort of agreement. I want to buy those guns from you."

"What about your stepdaughter?"

"What about her?"

"Technically these guns are hers. They are a part of her shipment."

"No, they're not," Crowder said. "Her shipment got blown up in the bushwhacker's attack. These guns are yours and she don't even come into the picture. I'm willing to buy them from you."

"How much?"

"One hundred-and-twenty-five dollars," Crowder said.

"Why are you being so generous to me?" Morgan asked. "That's more than you offered Miss Chapel. Why not raise the offer to her?"

"Oh, for a very good reason," Crowder said,

smiling confidently. He leaned back in his chair and folded his arms across his chest. "I want you to tell her that you sold the guns to me for seventy-five dollars each. When she realizes that you have undersold her, she'll be forced to come down in price in order to do business."

"What makes you think I would do such a thing?"

"Because, Mr. Morgan, in the short run, it's good business. In the long run, it will even be good for Miss Chapel. She'll sell her guns at a fair profit . . . not a gougers' profit mind you, but at a fair profit. And, she'll have a foothold in Dawson for her guns."

"It's good to see that you are looking out for everyone," Morgan said.

Crowder chuckled. "Well, like I told Miss Chapel, there's plenty enough money up here for all of us to get rich, if we just don't get too greedy over it. Now, what do you say? Do we have a deal?"

Morgan stroked his chin for a moment, then nodded. "Yeah, Crowder," he said. "We've got a deal."

"Good, good," Crowder said, rubbing his hands together eagerly. "Now, how many guns do you have? And what kind are they?"

"Remington Frontier .44s," Morgan said.

"Ah, yes, just like the Peacemaker."

"They don't have as good a balance," Morgan said.

"Well, you should know. But believe me, Morgan, I could sell flintlock pistols up here."

"I'm sure you would."

Crowder laughed. "Oh, yes, I would if I had them. Now, how many of these guns do you have?"

"Twenty five."

"Let's see, that would be $3,125," Crowder said. "All right, Mr. Morgan, you deliver the pistols to me and I'll pay you, cash on delivery."

"You'll have them by nine o'clock," Morgan said. He started to get up from his seat when a big, meaty hand suddenly, and roughly, pushed him back down into the chair.

"No! You no cheat Lady Boss!" Chotauk said.

"You stay the hell out of this, you goddamned Eskimo!" Crowder shouted, standing up across the table.

Chotauk brushed Morgan aside as if he were no more than a fly and went after Crowder. Crowder didn't give ground and the two men met in the middle of the table which had suddenly turned into kindling wood.

Chotauk drove a right into Crowder's jaw, knocking him back against the wall. Though a large man himself, Crowder wasn't quite as large as Chotauk, but he did have a leathery toughness about him, and he was a man who had been tried many times so that he was a skilled barroom fighter. He also had a killer instinct, and such an instinct served him exceptionally well in a fight where there were no rules.

Crowder drove a low, whistling right into Chotauk's groin, catching him by surprise and numbing him with the ferocity of the blow to his balls. Chotauk let out a bellow of pain and dropped both hands to protect himself. Crowder smiled, confidently. He was confident, but he was no fool. He knew he would have to get in a telling blow quickly, so while Chotauk was still doubled over in pain, Crowder slammed a fist into Chotauk's Adam's apple. Chotauk staggered back toward the bar and Crowder followed him, hitting him two more times with blows that would stun a buffalo. Finally, Chotauk went down to his knees, so far having thrown only one blow . . . the first one of the fight.

"Come on, you big Eskimo, get up and fight!" some of the crowd shouted.

"Finish 'im off, Big Ben," others encouraged.

In fact, very few cared who won the fight. They were watching it as a diversion and bets were rapidly placed as if this were a match put on by the gaming commission.

News of the fight spread fast and more than a dozen new men rushed in through the door to see the collision of the two giants.

Crowder, intending to make quick work of Chotauk, drew back for one final, telling blow to put him away. Though Crowder had gotten the upper hand, temporarily, Chotauk wasn't out of it, and he saw Crowder get set for a roundhouse right. At the last possible instant, Chotauk jerked his head to one side. Crowder's hand slid past and slammed hard into the bar, crashing through the front and temporarily holding him, like a bear with its paw caught in a trap. That gave Chotauk the opportunity to send a short, brutal right into Crowder's belly, drawing a loud grunt and knocking Crowder loose from the bar, sending him backwards with quick little steps to keep him from falling down. Chotauk used that opportunity to jump to his feet.

By now Crowder realized that he had lost his advantage. His only hope over the big Eskimo had been to take him out by surprise, but Chotauk had taken everything Crowder could dish out and was now coming at him on even terms. Desperately, Crowder sent a left jab toward Chotauk, but Chotauk slipped it easily and countered with a short right hook to Crowder's jaw. It was only the third time Chotauk had swung at Crowder, but all three punches had landed with telling effectiveness.

Crowder tried another left jab, hoping to set Chotauk up for a roundhouse right. Chotauk took the jab in order to get in close. He hooked Crowder with a left, then caught him flush with a hard right, and Crowder went down.

"Get up, Big Ben. Get up!" some of his supporters were yelling. "Get up, get up!"

Crowder struggled to his feet, then reached for a chair. Raising it over his head he started for Chotauk. Chotauk stood his ground. He had a clear, unobstructed shot at Crowder's jaw, and he put everything into a roundhouse right which lifted Crowder from the floor, then sent him crashing through another table. Crowder lay on the floor with his mouth open, his jaws slack, and his eyes closed, totally unconscious.

"Holy shit, did you see that?" someone asked.

"You reckon he broke his neck?"

"Naw, look at the bastard. He's sleepin' like a dog in the sun."

Chotauk looked over at Morgan and pointed at him. "You no cheat Boss Lady," he said. "We go get guns, bring them to town, sell them ourselves."

•

17

Skagway Annie stood at the window of her room, Room 212 of the Klondike Hotel, and looked down on Main Street. A few minutes earlier she had seen several people running across the street to the North Star Hotel and she sent Cole and Pascal to find out what was going on.

The three of them had arrived this morning. They came to Dawson when Annie found out that was where Mariellen Chapel had gone. She had a score to settle with the bitch who called herself the Queen of the Klondike, and if she had to follow her to hell to take care of it, she was willing to do so. So far, Mariellen didn't know she was here, and that was the way she intended to keep it. She heard a pounding on the door and walked over to open it. Cole and Pascal were standing on the other side.

"Well, did you find out what was going on?" she asked.

"Yeah. There was one hell of a fight," Cole said.

"I thought it might be something like that,"

Annie said. "Well, that's none of our concern. What we need to do is find out where—"

"You might be interested in it," Cole interrupted. "It was between that big Eskimo that follows Miss Chapel around all the time, and a fella they call Big Ben Crowder."

"Yeah," Pascal said. "And it was over guns. Lots of guns."

Annie smiled. "Really? It could be that our luck is changing," she said. "What did you find out?"

The two gunmen told of the conversation they had overheard between Morgan and Crowder . . . about the guns that were hidden somewhere. And they told of the big Eskimo's challenge to Morgan.

"That's what he said? That he and Mariellen would get the guns and bring them in to sell themselves?" Annie asked.

"That's what he said."

Annie's eyes flashed with excitement, and she walked back over to the window to look down on the town again.

"Well, now, ain't that a lucky break for us? Looks to me like we're gonna kill two birds with one stone. We can follow Queenie and her polar bear out to where they have the guns, take care of them, and get the guns."

"How do you want to take care of them?"

Annie looked around from the window. "Take care of them," she said coldly, but without elaboration.

The two gunmen looked at each other and smiled. Further elaboration wasn't needed. Annie turned back to the window and her eyes grew cold and distant. "I'll teach that bitch to burn me out," she said.

* * *

When Chotauk and Mariellen drove their dog team through the middle of Dawson, there wasn't a person in the entire town who didn't know where they were going. And there were quite a few who gave a passing thought to following them, to discovering for themselves where the treasure trove of guns was hidden. Rumors had been flying about town ever since she arrived, and some were saying there were as many as one-thousand guns buried in the snow out there, though how one-thousand guns could have been brought up on one dog sled, no one stopped to consider.

They did stop to consider whether or not they wanted to follow her out though. The ones who hadn't actually witnessed the fight between Chotauk and Crowder had heard of it, and no one wanted to go up against Miss Mariellen Chapel's bodyguard.

No one, that is, except the two gunman who were being paid by Skagway Annie Thompson to follow, and take care of, Mariellen Chapel and her bodyguard. And, in the process, bring back the guns.

Cole and Pascal waited a full half hour before they left with their own team. They left casually, heading east, as if they were going up into one of the Indian villages to trade for pelts. Mariellen and Chotauk had been heading south when they left town, so Cole and Pascal were positive that the different directions would throw off anyone of a suspicious nature.

No more than a mile out of town, Cole and Pascal turned south. They were both experienced dog sledders and they felt that by pushing their team, they would quickly cut the trail of the people they were following. They would stay back, far enough that they were completely out of sight, so Mariellen and Chotauk wouldn't suspect they were being followed. That way there would be no hesitancy about getting the guns. It wouldn't be very productive to catch up with them before they got to the guns, because then they would lose out.

Morgan had built a snow shelter and he was waiting in it, wrapped in caribou robes to keep warm. He heard the dogs approaching and he stood up to meet them.

"Anyone following?" he asked.

"I don't know," Chotauk answered. "I see no one."

"Maybe no one came," Mariellen suggested.

"Don't say that," Morgan said. "That would mean we put on that little show for nothing."

"Wait," Chotauk said, holding up his hand. "I hear dogs."

The three of them were silent for a long moment, then Morgan heard it, the long, thin yap of dogs on the trail.

"All right," Morgan said. "Someone did take the bait. You know what to do?"

"Yes," Mariellen said. "We'll be digging in the snow over there, while you're hidden out here."

"Right."

"Lee, I don't suppose I have to remind you that we're depending on you to not let anything happen, do I?"

Morgan chuckled. "Doesn't it make you wish you had been nicer to me when we first met?"

The barks grew louder and Mariellen and

Chotauk hurried over to put on their act. There were, of course, no guns at all. The *argument* between Chotauk and Morgan had merely been to call attention to the suggestion that there were guns, and Chotauk's assertion that he and Mariellen would bring the guns in to sell themselves was to see who they could get to fall into their trap. Now, it appeared that someone was about to do so.

Morgan hurried into a place of concealment, being careful to take a wide route around so that footprints would not give away his position. He waited until the uncoming dog sled approached.

There were two men on the sled, but they were so bundled up that Morgan couldn't see them well enough to identify them, even if he knew them. As the sled approached, one of them pushed down on the brake, a little spade device that dug into the snow, and the sled stopped. Chotauk and Mariellen looked around at them.

"Well, now, lookie here what we have," one of the two men said. "If it ain't the Queen of the Klondike and her pet polar bear."

"Cole, Pascal," Mariellen said. She said the names loud enough for Morgan to hear them, warning him in that way that these weren't just a couple of sourdoughs out to make an easy dollar. These were professional gunfighters. "What are you doing up here? I thought you were down in Skagway."

"Yeah? What would we be doing down there?" Cole asked angrily. "You burned half the goddamned town before you left."

"Yes, I do seem to recall a fire," Mariellen said.

"Have you dug 'em up yet?" Pascal asked, pointing to the snow.

"Dug what up?" Mariellen asked innocently.

"Look, sister, don't play dumb with us. We know you come out here lookin' for the guns you got hid. So be a nice girl an' dig 'em up for us."

Chotauk took a step toward the two men and they both had their guns out, amazingly fast considering the fact that they were so bundled up against the cold.

"Tell the polar bear to stop or we'll see how many bullets it takes to stop him," Pascal growled.

"Chotauk," Mariellen said quietly.

The big Eskimo stopped.

Pascal grinned. "Yeah, I like to see that. I like it the way you have him trained."

"Don't judge Chotauk by yourselves," Mariellen said. "He's a loyal friend. He's not a lap dog the way you two are to Annie Thompson."

"Yeah, well he's gonna be a dead friend if he takes another step. Now, dig up them guns."

"There are no guns."

"Don't give me that. Ever'one in town is talkin' about 'em. Now dig 'em up and load 'em on the sled. And be quick about it, we ain't got all day."

"I told you, there aren't any guns."

"And I told you to quit lyin' to me. Load 'em up."

"She isn't lying," Morgan suddenly said, appearing behind the two men.

"What the?" Cole asked, spinning around with his revolver in his hand.

"No, don't," Morgan shouted, and he pointed his pistol right at Cole's head. "Unless you want to be dead."

"Cole, remember them two wood parrots he shot?" Pascal warned.

"Yeah," Cole growled. "I remember."

"I'm glad you remember," Morgan said. "I'm even better at shooting lap dogs."

Mariellen and Chotauk both laughed.

"The lady was right, you know," Morgan went on. "There are no guns."

"But I don't understand. Why have you been tellin' ever'one you had guns out here?"

"We were just baiting the trap to see who we would catch," Mariellen said. She smiled, prettily. "And look who came waltzing in."

"Yeah," Morgan said. "The only thing is, we set bait for a fox and we caught a couple of weasels."

"You mean you don't think they are the ones?"

"No. They aren't smart enough to be the ones we're after."

"But they work for Skagway Annie. If's she's not smart enough, nobody is," Mariellen protested.

"Oh, I agree, Annie is smart enough, all right. But she's not the one we're after. My guess is these boys were after something entirely different from our mastermind."

"Just what were you going to do out here?" Mariellen asked.

"We was supposed to take care of you then bring the guns back to Miss Thompson," Cole said.

"Cole, shut the hell up," Pascal ordered. "You don't have to blabber everything you know."

"I don't intend to take the rap all by myself," Cole defended.

"When did you three arrive from Skagway?" Morgan asked.

"Yesterday," Cole said.

"Can you prove that?" Mariellen asked.

"Prove it? No," Cole said. He looked confused. "I don't understand, why the hell should I have to prove when I got here? There ain't no law against comin' up here if I want to."

"Do you believe him?" Mariellen asked.

"Yes," Morgan said. "He's too goddamned dumb to lie about it."

"What do we do with them?"

"Chotauk, get their guns," Morgan said. "About the only thing we can do is send them back."

"You can't take our guns away from us," Pascal complained. "You can't turn us lose up here with no way to defend ourselves."

"Why you two no account bastards," Morgan said. "There are more people up here without guns than there are with. And by taking your guns away from you we've made those people a lot safer."

Chotauk took the guns, then looked at the two disarmed men and laughed. "Too bad we not learn," he said.

"Learn? Learn what?"

"How many bullets you can put in polar bear, before polar bear kill you," Chotauk said easily.

18

"And nobody showed up?"

"Only the two hardcases that work for Skagway Annie," Morgan said. "And I don't think they are the ones we're after."

"Don't you think they are capable of killing?" Constable Bannister asked.

"Oh, yes, not only capable, but I'm certain they've done their share," Morgan said. "It's just that they aren't behind all of this, and neither is Skagway Annie."

"That leaves us right back where we started," Bannister said.

"Not quite, I have a few bumps and bruises I didn't have when all this started," Crowder said with a chuckle.

"Well, you said it yourself, Ben, you wanted to make the fight as real as possible," Morgan said.

"Yes, well, I guess I said that because I thought I could whip him. It's all right to make the fight real if I'm going to win. But if I'm going to lose, that's something else again."

Both Morgan and Bannister laughed at

Crowder's observation.

"I'm sorry I couldn't tell you earlier that Crowder was the one who tried to get the report to you," Bannister said. "Of course, since it was all unofficial, that was the only way it could be done."

"It was all arranged," Crowder went on. "Bannister let me know by a certain signal that he would be gone from the office for five minutes. That was all the time I needed to sneak in and get the report."

"And the envelope it came in?"

"That was easy," Crowder said. "I got it from my stepson's files. Then I put the report in the envelope, dropped that in another envelope, and mailed it to you."

"Why did you use another envelope?"

"Simple. I didn't want anyone seeing the RCMP seal on the outside envelope, because if the wrong person saw it, it would be a simple matter for them to intercept it. I included the RCMP envelope so you would realize that the report was authentic."

"Of course, what we didn't anticipate was that someone intercepted your mail anyway," Bannister explained. "They opened it, took out the RCMP envelope, then took out the report that was inside, and slipped the RCMP envelope under your door."

"That's what I don't understand," Crowder said. "Why didn't they take all of it? Why did they give him the envelope?"

"It was probably just their way of having some fun with me," Morgan said. "But it backfired on them because it has led me this far, and now I've read the report they didn't want me to see."

"Yes," Bannister said. "You can imagine my

surprise when the report turned up in my mail a short while later. I didn't know what to do about it, so I merely put it back in the original envelope . . . although, of course, it now had creases, as you so cleverly observed."

"Frank Church," Morgan said. "It all boils down to who he is . . . and where he is."

"Yes, well, I've been thinking about that," Bannister said. "Have you ever considered synonyms, Mr. Morgan?"

"Synonyms?"

"Yes, synonyms. Sometimes a clever criminal when constructing a new identity for himself, will—"

"Constable! Constable, come quick!"

Bannister stood up and moved quickly to the door of his little office. "What is it?" he asked.

"There's a couple of galoots in the North Star gettin' awful nasty. They done shot one man, an' they're layin' the claim that blood's gonna run in the streets before they're through."

"What has them so riled up?" Bannister asked.

"Somethin' about how many bullets it takes to kill a polar bear."

Morgan stood up quickly when he heard that. "Constable, you'd better let me handle this," he said. "That's Cole and Pascal, and the polar bear they're riled up over is Chotauk."

"No, thank you, Mr. Morgan," Bannister said. He strapped his black leather belt and pistol holster on. As usual, the flap was buttoned down on the holster.

"But I know these men," Morgan said. "They are gunfighters."

"They are violators of the law, Mr. Morgan, and as such, are subject to my jurisdiction."

Morgan watched Bannister leave the office and walk swiftly, purposefully, toward the splash of yellow light that was the North Star Saloon.

"Surely he'll take out that pistol before he gets in there," Morgan observed.

"I don't think so," Crowder said.

Morgan looked at Crowder in disbelief. "You mean he'll walk right in there with his gun still in his holster to make the arrest?"

"He's a man that believes in the power of the law," Crowder said.

"Yeah? Well he's going up against two men who believe only in the power of the gun," Morgan replied. He pushed out into the street and started toward the saloon.

"Hey, wait, where are you goin'?" Crowder called. "Bannister won't let you interfere with his arrest."

Cole and Pascal were armed again, thanks to Skagway Annie. She berated them for their failure, and for losing their weapons, but she couldn't very well have bodyguards who were unarmed, so she paid $150 apiece for two Colt .44 Peacemakers. They were the same kind of pistols Cole and Pascal lost, so they were glad to get them back. They were so glad they began celebrating, and a few minutes ago the celebration had erupted into a shooting. Now one man lay bleeding on the floor and everyone else in the saloon was backed up against the walls, giving Cole and Pascal all the room they needed.

"Well, now, lookie here, will you, Pascal?" Cole said, deriding all the customers of the saloon. "There's not one man in town . . . not one man who'll step up to the bar with us and have a drink."

"They're yellow bellies," Pascal said, laughing. He took a drink of whiskey straight from the bottle and looked at everyone who was cowering against the wall. He made an imaginary pistol with his thumb and forefinger, then made a shooting sound with his mouth. The man he pointed his hand at shrank back in fear.

"Ha, ha! Look at that!" Pascal laughed, pointing at the frightened customer.

"Bartender, I thought you had men up here," Cole said. "You got nothing up here but yellow bellies and old women."

"Yeah, only old women got more guts than these yellow bellies," Pascal said. He "shot" another customer with his imaginary gun.

The front door opened then and a well groomed man of medium height stepped into the room. He wasn't wearing a fur hat like everyone else, he was wearing a blocked hat with a golden crest on the crown. Though he was wearing a parka, his red coat could be seen underneath, and he wore black pants with a red stripe down the legs. A pistol belt was fastened around his waist and a pistol, secured by a holster flap, was at his side.

"Well, now, gentlemen, that's quite enough, don't you think? I'm Constable Bannister."

Bannister heard a quiet groan and he looked at a man lying on the floor. When he looked around the room he recognized one of the town doctors.

"Doc, how about taking a look at this injured man?"

"I started to a moment ago," the doctor replied. "But they pulled a gun on me and made me get back."

"Really, gentlemen, you would deny an injured man medical attention? See to him, Doc."

"But they—"

"See to him, Doc," Bannister said again. "The law will attend to these two. You gentlemen surrender your firearms to me, now. You are under arrest."

Cole and Pascal looked at each other in momentary confusion, then they both burst out laughing.

"Arrest? You are putting us under arrest?" Cole said.

"Yes," Bannister said. "Oh, I assure you, gentlemen, you won't find it so amusing when you spend thirty years in one of our jails for attempted homicide."

"Attempted what?" Cole asked.

"It means attempted killin'," Pascal explained.

Cole laughed again. "Oh, we wasn't attemptin' to kill the sonofabitch," he said. "If we had really been tryin' to do it, we would'a done it."

"Yes. Well, nevertheless, you are both under arrest. Please surrender your firearms at once."

Cole pointed to the constable. "Mister, you're talkin' like somebody that ain't go no sense. Here you are with your gun in that shiny holster an' a flap down over it, tellin' us to give you our guns? Why, don't you know we could blow you to hell before you could even get your hand to the holster?"

"I am the law," Bannister said. "And I am ordering you to surrender your firearms."

"And I'm tellin' you we ain't gonna do it," Cole said.

"Very well, I can see that it will be necessary for me to enforce the demand," Bannister said.

He reached for the flap and unbuttoned it.

"Don't go reachin' for that gun, mister, 'cause if you do, law or no law, we're gonna have to shoot you," Pascal warned.

"I'm sorry," Bannister said. "But the law is quite specific about this. Now you are going to have to surrender your weapons at once." Bannister started to withdraw his pistol.

"I told you not to do that!" Cole yelled.

Undaunted, Bannister continued his slow, methodical withdrawal.

Guns appeared in the hands of both Cole and Pascal at nearly the same instant. Almost as quickly as the guns were in their hands, they were firing, and a billow of smoke pushed out from the barrels of the two Peacemakers.

Bannister was hit by both bullets and they slammed him back against the bar. He put his elbows back, trying to hold onto the bar, trying to stay up, but he couldn't do it. With a look of surprise on his face he slowly slid to the floor.

Morgan stepped through the door of the saloon just as Bannister slid down. The constable was in the sitting position and he looked up at Morgan with an expression of disbelief on his face. Morgan knelt on the floor beside the young constable.

"They defied the law," he said. "Don't they understand? Without the law we are nothing but barbarians." Bannister leaned his head back and closed his eyes. He took a few deep breaths, then opened his eyes again. "Barbarians," he said, then, with a sigh, he died.

Morgan looked back at Cole and Pascal, both of whom still held smoking guns in their hands.

"Did you see him?" Pascal said, pointing at the

dead lawman. "He was crazy. He started pulling his pistol against us, even when we warned him."

"It wasn't him pulling the pistol," Morgan said. "It was the law."

Cole laughed, derisively. "The law?" he said. He shook his head. "What the hell is this law? There's only one law up here and I'm holdin' it right in my hand." Cole raised the pistol for Morgan to see it.

Morgan was still on one knee beside the constable. "You heard the man," Morgan said. "Without the law, we are barbarians. Now, I'm going to ask you to do what he said. I'm going to ask you to turn over your guns."

"Goddamnit, man, at least when he asked, our guns were in our holster. Now they're in our hands. You're crazier than he was."

"Oh, no, there's one major difference between the constable and me," Morgan said.

"Yeah. What's that?"

"The constable believed in the power and authority of law. He believed that was all he needed to keep the peace. I don't believe that."

"What do you believe?"

"I think the only way I'm going to keep the peace with the two of you is to kill both of you," Morgan said.

Several of the onlookers gasped in amazement at the man who, on his knee, and with his pistol in its holster, had just threatened to kill two men who had their pistols in their hands.

"You're . . . you're crazy," Cole said. He made a cackling sound that might have been a laugh.

"This is the last time I'm going to tell you," Morgan said. "Put your guns on the table there, or I'm going to kill both of you, right here and right now."

"Try it," Pascal hissed.

Morgan had his pistol out so fast that most people were aware only of a jerk in the shoulder. He fired two shots, so fast, and so close together, that people in the building next door thought they heard one shot . . . or at least, two guns going off simultaneously. There wasn't two guns going off at the same time, or even two guns going off at all. Morgan shot twice, neither Cole nor Pascal fired a shot. Both men were dead before they even realized what had happened.

"My God!" Crowder gasped. "I've never seen anything like that in my life!" Crowder had followed Morgan into the saloon, arriving just as the constable died. "What man can draw and shoot that fast?"

"I can," Morgan said, standing up and holstering his pistol. He looked down at the two men he had just killed, at the surprise on their faces. Then he turned away from them and left the saloon, pushing past the stare of the awed onlookers, walking out into the street to let the cold air clear his senses. He walked down the middle of the snow packed street, listening to the babble of voices in the saloon behind him, knowing they were talking about him, but purposely blotting out any specific words. He didn't want to hear praise right now, he didn't want to hear anything except the peaceful sigh of the night wind.

Morgan knew what nobody in the saloon knew. He hadn't killed the two men in a fair fight, though to everyone there it not only looked fair, it looked like the odds were tipped against him. It wasn't a fair fight at all.

Morgan didn't understand the technical terms for it, had never even heard the word reflex, but he knew that if someone was holding a gun on him and didn't start to pull the trigger until they saw Morgan begin to draw, they would never get the trigger pulled. For the longest part of a draw was the part where the brain thought about it, then told the arm, hand, and finger to move. Morgan's arm, hand, and finger were already moving. Before the message got from Cole and Pascal's brain to their fingers, telling the finger to pull the trigger, it was too late. Morgan had already shot them. They would be telling stories to their grandchildren about this gun battle, Morgan knew. He wondered how long it would be before anyone figured out that it wasn't a gun battle . . . it was an execution.

19

Harder and harder, again and again, Morgan lunged into her. Mariellen's hair, soaked with the sweat of their passion, lay pasted to the trembling mounds of her chest, half crushed beneath him. Her passion was building faster and faster, her turgid nipples digging into Morgan's flesh as she writhed in ecstasy.

Mariellen suddenly choked back a little scream of pleasure, then bit him on the shoulder. His hands searched her body, raking up and down her back to hold and squeeze her pounding buttocks. Her hands went to his head, her teeth chewing on his lower lip, her body writhing like a snake.

Morgan continued to drink the nectar of her lips as she thrashed and heaved beneath him. His own groans of ecstasy were absorbed by her hot mouth as she opened it wide and sucked his lips, crushing them with her teeth and inflaming them with her rapier tongue.

They clung to each other, kissing wildly, their hands searching, grasping, clutching, finding, tearing at each other, hers as eager as his. Her moans came steadily, her back arched, carrying him with her. He lunged harder against her, redoubling every ounce of effort he had left. His surge tore a wild cry from her as she bit him again. His body slammed to hers over and over until she cried out, "Now! Now!" and her throbbing hips arched upward as she tightened her legs around him. She flung her head back, her wild hair flowing past her shoulder, while her lower torso undulated, bucked, and jerked its harsh rhythm.

Morgan approached the ultimate moment, cupping her upthrust breasts, squeezing them unmercifully. He sighed, stiffening, as salvo after salvo of hot sperm spurted out. She gurgled and cried out his name and her features, which had been frozen by the agony of lust, softened and her lips parted. "That was wonderful," she said. "Just wonderful."

Mariellen stood by the window of the bedroom, looking out at the snow. Though a roaring fire in the little stove kept the room pleasantly warm, she was holding a blanket around her nude body. The blanket stopped at her waist and her naked thighs gleamed in the soft light. A breast peaked through the blanket's fold, its nipple still congested. She had been silent for a long moment, then she turned toward him. Her eyes were glistening with tears, one had started down her cheek, leaving a streak behind it.

"You won't come back to Skagway with Chotauk and me?"

"Not yet," Morgan said.

"But there's no need to stay up here now," she said. "Everyone knows who we are. They know we don't have any guns. Even if there is someone to catch, we have no bait for the trap."

"They aren't going to send a new constable in here until after the ice breaks up," Morgan said.

"But I don't understand. What's that to you?"

"I know you don't understand," Morgan said. "I'm not sure I understand myself. But I want to watch over things for Bannister. There was something about that funny little man . . . his insistance that we must be governed by laws . . . that got to me."

"You'll come down to Skagway in the spring?"

"Yes," Morgan said. "In the spring, I promise."

"All right," she said. She sighed. "It will probably be that long before we can get another shipment of weapons up here anyway."

"Tell Chotauk I thank him for letting me live here."

Mariellen suddenly smiled. "It's not Chotauk you need to thank. It's me. I could be very jealous, you know, leaving you here with another woman."

Morgan thought of the woman Mariellen was talking about, Chotauk's wife, as pie faced, bland, and round as any woman he had ever seen. He chuckled. "I'll say this about her. I've never known anyone who was a better cook. I may be as big as Chotauk by the time I come back."

The trip downriver was a lot easier than the trip Morgan had made upriver five months earlier. He stood on the desk of the *Maid of the Klondike,* a riverboat that served Dawson and Whitehorse, watching the water froth into foam behind the paddle. The ice was gone from the river, thousands of wild flowers bloomed in colorful profusion on both sides of the Yukon, patches of green fed the caribou and other foragers, while overhead the sun warmed the air to a balmy sixty-five degrees.

It was good to be out of the parkas and furs, to dress normally for a change. And it was good to get out of Dawson, though Morgan had to confess that the winter he had just spent was the most unique winter of his entire lifetime.

"Mr. Morgan, the dining room will be closing for the night soon," one of the crewmen told him. "If you haven't taken your supper, this is your last chance."

"Thanks," Morgan said. He looked out at the crystal clear sky, as bright as midday though it was already nine o'clock in the evening. He had just gotten used to living in constant darkness . . . now he would have to make the same accommodations for constant light. He left the deck and went to take his supper.

He bought a horse in Whitehorse and rode the animal through the Chilkoot Pass to Skagway. It was a much easier trip this time than it had been before, and days before he thought it was possible, he found himself descending the mountain trail into the coastal town of Skagway.

This was the first time he had ever seen Skagway without its mantle of snow. Without the element's softening effect, Skagway was a raw, rough, frontier town, a place of mucky streets and plank sidewalks. It's population was near ten thousand people now, and swelling every day as new prospectors came to the established gold fields, or flocked together to be fleeced like sheep by a coalition of corrupt government officials and hoodlums. Most of them poured off the ships and headed for the Klondike laden with supplies brought from the States . . . and many of these were murdered between the mud flats called Skagway Beach and the summit of White Pass.

The guns which were at such a premium in the interior of Alaska, or the Northwest Territories, were in more common supply here as the men brought their own. As a result of the accessibility to the guns, shootings were routine and armed robberies on the streets were common. This was, Morgan realized, frontier country, as real and as rugged as anything his father had faced in an earlier generation. Here, for the first time since coming to Alaska, Morgan felt in charge of his own environment. In a world where the gun was law, Morgan could argue his case in any court in the land, up to and including the Supreme Court.

Morgan rode by what had been Thompson's Cove. He knew it had burned down last winter, but he didn't know it had been replaced by another saloon. He dismounted, tied his horse off at the hitching rail in front, then walked across the boards to avoid the mud and went inside.

"We got some beer fresh in from the States," the bartender said.

"Sounds good," Morgan agreed. He looked around the saloon. Though functional, it certainly had none of the class of the old Thompson's Cove. "Miss Thompson around?"

"Who?" the bartender asked, setting a mug in front of Morgan.

"Thompson. Annie Thompson."

"No," the bartender said, his face drawn in confusion. Then it changed into recognition. "Say, are you talkin' about he woman they used to call Skagway Annie?"

"Yes."

"No, she ain't in Skagway anymore. I heard tell she went up to Nome, but I wouldn't know nothin' about it. She was gone long before I come here. She's just one of them stories you hear the old timers tellin' all the time," he said.

Morgan took a drink of his beer. My god, was he now considered an "old timer" up here?

"What they like to do," the bartender went on, "is take somebody just arrived . . . like you, say, an' fill his head with all sorts of tales. Don't believe none of it. Take this here Skagway Annie, for example. They're tellin' a story now 'bout the two gunfighters she always had with her, how they was kilt by one of them mounties. And get this . . . the story goes that they was two of 'em with the drop on the mountie, but he drawned his gun and kilt 'em both before they could even pull the trigger. Now if that ain't the beatenist story you ever heard?"

"I knew that mounted policeman," Morgan said. "His name was Bannister . . . and the story is true."

"Go on," the bartender said. "They ain't nobody that fast." Noticing Morgan had finished the beer he went on. "Care for another one?"

"Thanks, no," Morgan said. "I've got some business to tend to."

When Morgan tied his horse at the hitching rail in front of the Queen's Throne, Chotauk came out onto the porch to greet him. He smiled broadly and stuck out his hand.

"Well, Chotauk," Morgan said. "Your woman sends greetings."

"And my friend, Crowder?"

"Yes," Morgan said. "Your friend Crowder sends greetings as well."

"Boss Lady wait for you inside," Chotauk said,

holding the door open for him.

The Queen's Throne was crowded with customers, and as Morgan looked over them he was surprised to see how easily he could pick out the newcomers from the old sourdoughs. No wonder everyone who spoke to him last year knew immediately that he was a tenderfoot. From the clothes they wore, the language they used, even their very demeanor, it was as easy to determine who just got off the boat as if they were wearing large signs advertising the fact.

When Morgan started up the stairs to Mariellen's office, two armed men moved quickly to intercept him.

"Out of my way, clowns," Morgan growled, "or I'll break the two of you into little pieces."

"I'd like to see you try that, mister," one of them said.

"No, I don't think you would," a woman's voice called down from the top of the stairs. "This is Lee Morgan and if he says he can break you into little pieces, I'm sure he can."

Both of the guards backed away quickly.

"I'm sorry, Miss Mariellen," one of them said. "I didn't recognize him."

"No reason you should," Mariellen replied. "You've never seen him before. Well," she called down to him, "are you going to come up, or do I have to come down for you?"

Morgan smiled up at her, recalling her aloofness when he first arrived last fall. "No, I'll come up to you," he said. "I certainly wouldn't want to cause people to talk."

"I don't care if anyone talks or not," Mariellen said, laughing happily. She came halfway down the stairs and plastered herself against him with a long kiss. Her two armed guards looked away in embarrassment and, Morgan noticed, not a little envy. "Come on up to my office," she said. "We've got a lot to talk about."

In the office Mariellen poured Morgan a glass of wine, then curled up on a sofa beside him and listened as he told her of the winter spent in Dawson, and of the newly arrived constable.

"He's older than Bannister, and maybe a little more practical. I think he'll do just fine."

"And you and Big Ben kept the peace all winter," she said. "I thought you were dead set against wearing a badge."

"Oh, I didn't wear a badge," Morgan said. "And I had no official position . . . neither did Crowder, for that matter. I guess that's why I was able to do it without it going against my grain. In fact, the only thing that has stuck in my craw all winter is I still don't know who tried to have me ambushed when I went up there, and I still don't know who the mysterious Mr. Church is. When you come right down to it, I guess I didn't do that good of a job for Colt Firearms."

"Oh, that reminds me," Mariellen said. "I have a letter for you from Colt Firearms Company. I was told to hold it for your arrival." Mariellen got up from the sofa, looked through a little case, then brought him an envelope. "It came two weeks ago," she said.

"What's in it?"

"I don't know. As you can see it's marked personal and confidential. I didn't look."

Morgan opened the envelope and pulled out the letter. It was dated six weeks ago.

Dear Mr. Morgan,

Two-thirds of our board concurring, we are

hereby dismissing Harrison Chapel from all duties and responsibilities with our company. He is no longer our representative in Alaska, or the Northwest Territories, and is not authorized to speak for us in any capacity.

The reasons for his dismissal are of a confidential nature. The original terms of your own employment are still in effect, should you wish to continue working for us. We would also like to offer you the position once held by Mr. Chapel, and now void. Should you accept that position, you will then be told why we found it necessary to terminate Chapel's employment. In any case, whether you continue in your present capacity, or accept our offer of new responsibilities, you are no longer answerable to Mr. Harrison Chapel for any business regarding Colt Firearms.

"Has your uncle said anything to you about his work with the Colt Company?" Morgan asked.

"Do you mean do I know he has quit? Yes, I know."

"Why?"

"I asked him the same question," Mariellen said. "After all, he had been with Colt for a number of years and I was quite surprised when he told me about it."

"What was his answer?"

"He said why have a sandwich when he can enjoy the entire banquet."

"I see."

"Well, if you do see, I wish you would tell me. I swear, that doesn't make one bit of sense to me."

"It would if you understood synonyms," Morgan said simply.

20

"Well," Chapel said, greeting Morgan when he went to his office to see him. "So, you've come down from the frozen north to visit us."

"Yes."

"Mariellen told me a little of what happened to you . . . how you were ambushed on the trail up, hit on the head, and shot it out with Cole and Pascal. I must say, you've had quite some experiences since signing on with Colt Firearms."

"I hope that doesn't mean I'm going to have even more experiences now," Morgan said.

Chapel looked at him in puzzlement for a moment, then nodded in understanding. "You're talking about the situation between Colt and me, aren't you?" He opened the humidor and extracted a cigar, offering one to Morgan.

Morgan accepted. "Yeah. I received a letter from them."

"Well," Chapel said, biting the tip off his cigar, then holding a match to it. After his was lit, he held the match out to the end of Morgan's smoke.

"I suppose it's time you and I had a little talk, isn't it?"

"I suppose it is," Morgan said.

"No doubt Colt has told you why they fired me." Chapel took a deep puff, then blew out a cloud of blue smoke. "Fired me, after all these years of loyal service to them. Can you believe that?"

"I'd like to hear your side," Morgan said. Of course he hadn't even heard Colt's side yet, but Chapel evidently didn't realize that.

"Well, I told my niece I quit. I mean, I didn't want to tell her that a respectable company like Colt Firearms would do that to one of its most faithful employees."

It did not escape Morgan's notice that Chapel chose the word faithful over trusted.

"But it's all right that they fired me, I was going to quit sooner or later . . . I just thought it would make things go easier for me if I would continue to work for Colt as long as I could."

"But they wouldn't go along with that," Morgan said. It was a safe enough statement under the circumstances, and it helped to continue the illusion that he already knew why Colt had fired him.

"No," Chapel said. "They wouldn't go along with firearms exclusively . . . and any other dealings I might have with other companies was in violation of my contract. The fools."

Chapel's eyes narrowed in the smoke, but they gleamed brightly as he explained to Morgan his plans. "They are concerned with a few sales and protecting their name," he said. "They don't realize the money that could be made by controlling every firearm that comes up here. I don't mean just Colt arms, I'm talking about Remington, Winchester, Butterfield, Sharps, Deane and Adams, anybody you can think of. My God, there are few opportunities in a man's life when he can make a fortune . . . I mean a real fortune, like the monied giants back East, the Goulds, the Vanderbilts, the Mellons. I can be like one of them, Morgan, do you realize that? And all Colt is worried about is their precious name. They don't want to be involved in any scheme that would, in their words, 'defraud the public.' "

"Well, a respected name is a good thing to have," Morgan said.

"What the hell, you can buy a good name," Chapel said. "If I can pull this off, if I can make the money that I know is to be made up there, I can become a great friend of the people. One-hundred years from now there could be schools named for me like Vanderbilt, Stanford, and Cornell are named for their benefactors. Oh, yes, Morgan, I can buy my good name."

"I have to hand it to you, Chapel," Morgan said. "You do have ambition."

"What about you? Would you like to work with me? There's plenty of money up here for both of us."

"A full partner?" Morgan asked.

"Yeah, sure, a full partner. Why not?"

"Suppose I took you up on that offer?" Morgan asked. "What exactly would you expect of me?"

"The same thing I expected of you when we were working for Colt," Chapel said. "Morgan, the people who were killing off the Colt representatives, the people who tried to kill you, are still here, and the guns still make a tempting target for them, whether they are brought in by a large company like Colt, or by private enterprise such as ourselves. Quite simply I am buying your protection, just as Colt was."

"I see."

"Also," Chapel went on. "There is a shipment of guns at the docks in Juneau. I can't pick them up . . . I'm no longer a valid representative of the Colt Firearms Company. But you can."

"I suppose I can."

Chapel smiled broadly. "I knew we could do business together," he said. "I just knew it. Now, here's the plan. You pick up the Colt shipment and bring them to White Pass. I'll meet you there, and we'll take the guns on up into the gold fields. Morgan, they're paying over $200 each for them now."

"Two hundred dollars?"

"Yes. I knew that if we kept the guns out long enough the price would go up. That is exactly what I planned on. The only thing, I had thought to get the shipment from Colt before I quit. Well, no matter, you can get it for me, if you will."

"For money like that?" Morgan said. "Hell yes, I'll get them for you."

Chapel opened a cabinet and took out a bottle of brandy, then poured each of them a snifter. He held the drink out to Morgan.

"Let's have a drink to our partnership, partner, then you hurry on down there and get the guns. I'll meet you at White Pass in two weeks."

Morgan knew now that Alaska wasn't all glaciers and Yukon basin permafrost. The panhandle, warmed by the Japan Current, was no tropics, but in the summertime it would actually get balmy. Juneau was on the panhandle, the first boomtown of the Alaskan gold rush. It had sprouted beside a deep water channel beneath mountains where miners were routinely sluicing twenty-five dollars worth of gold a day.

Already tents and false fronted buildings had given way to the more substantial, more permanent structures, painted clapboard houses with shake roofs that would do credit to any town in New England.

In Juneau, Morgan took delivery of twenty cases of Colt .44 Peacemakers. Packed at twenty pistols a case, that was four hundred guns, which, at two-hundred dollars per gun, would make quite a sizeable start on Chapel's fortune. He transferred the guns to a boat going back up to Skagway, and three days later rode out of Skagway leading four pack mules.

Though the temperature in Skagway was warm enough to go about in shirtsleeves, White Pass, because of its elevation, was still covered with snow. Earlier travelers through the pass had broken a path of sorts, but there were still places where the snow came up to the chest of his animals, and sometimes Morgan had to dismount to lead them through. In a way it reminded him of the grueling dogsled journey he had made last year, only now he knew that when he came through on the other side it would be warm again.

And now he knew who his enemy was.

The first bullet could have killed him, but he had to take that chance . . . he had to expose himself until the other man made his move. Now the fat was in the fire. The bullet whistled by his head so close he could hear it passing by. He grabbed his rifle from the saddle boot and leaped off his horse into a snow bank alongside the trail. The snow bank wouldn't really turn aside a bullet, but it did provide him cover as he burrowed through it toward a nearby rock. He pulled himself up behind the rock, an apparition covered in snow, then peered out over the trail to see if he could spot his adversary.

It was bright out . . . a sparkling blue sky, a brilliant sun, and the bright glare of white snow. Morgan shielded his eyes and looked around.

"If you'll turn around and go on back . . . just leave the mules here, I might let you live," a voice called.

"Hello, Chapel," Morgan called back. "Or, should I say, Church?"

Morgan could hear Chapel laugh. "How long have you known?"

"Long enough that I knew better than to actually bring the guns with me," Morgan said. "There's nothing in the boxes."

"You don't really expect me to believe that, do you?" Chapel called back.

"See for yourself," Morgan said. "I'll send one of the mules through to you."

Morgan looked over at his pack mules, standing quietly by the trail. He aimed at the lead rope that connected the lead mule with the others, fired, and cut the rope with his shot. The mule bolted forward, running through the pass. Morgan watched until the animal reached the other side, then he saw a couple of men run out, grab the mule, and pull it off the trail.

"How many do you have with you?" Morgan asked.

"Enough to get the job done," Chapel

answered. There was a moment's pause, then Chapel yelled again. "Goddamnit, you're right! There's nothing in these boxes."

"I told you that, but you wouldn't listen," Morgan said.

"You should have followed the rules, Mr. Morgan. I don't like it when people don't follow the rules."

"What are you going to do about it?"

"Why, kill you, of course. I told you how big the stakes are in this game. I don't intend to let you do anything to mess it up."

Morgan looked up toward the head of the pass and saw five men moving toward him, darting swiftly from rock to rock, snowbank to snowbank, never giving him a clear shot. Five to one, he thought. Not very good odds.

A bullet suddenly hit the rock beside him, then whined off into the pass. Morgan turned on his side and saw three more coming down from a different direction. Now the odds were eight to one, and they were positioned so that if he took cover from one group, he was exposed to the other. He snapped off a shot at the three who were coming down from his side, then rolled away, just as the five men below opened up on him.

Bullets were popping into the snow all around him, kicking up little puffs to mark where they hit. Some of them were close . . . damned close.

Morgan heard something, a deep throated rumble, like thunder far in the distance. For a moment the sound surprised him . . . there wasn't a cloud in the sky. Where could the thunder have come from?

A bullet hit the rock right in front of him, and a

piece of chipped stone nicked his face, drawing blood. He heard the rumble again, and decided it was just distant echoes from the rifle fire. He raised up his head to see how close they were, then saw something that suddenly made all the rumblings clear. At the very top of the mountain he saw plumes of snow drifting off, evidence that there had just been a small snow slide. It wouldn't take too much to get the slide started in ernest.

High up on the slope behind Chapel and the others there was a tree loaded with heavy, wet, snow. Morgan raised his rifle to his shoulder and fired into the tree. His first bullet popped through harmlessly, but his second dislodged a pretty good sized snowball.

"What the hell?" he heard Chapel shout, when Chapel realized what Morgan was doing. "Morgan, you fool!"

Morgan fired a third time, and this time the shockwave of the bullet dumped half the tree's load into the snow. That, plus the sound of rifle fire that had already destabilized the snow, caused a large slide to begin. The slide grew larger, and larger still, until the entire side of the mountain started down, rolling up into a huge wave, roaring with the sound of a thousand cannons. Morgan had started a full fledged avalanche!

The eight men who had been steadily advancing toward him suddenly stopped in their tracks and looked back up the mountain toward the huge wall of snow rushing down at them with the speed of a runaway freight train. Morgan was struck with how tiny the men looked under these circumstances . . . they looked like toothpicks, like insignificant flies to be brushed away.

One of them may have screamed . . . Morgan believed he heard Chapel's voice, high and thin against the deep throated roar, but the voice, like the men themselves, was brushed away, snuffed out in an instant of terrible rolling, snapping, roaring white.

Morgan turned and dived back down the path. Falling and sliding, he was moving fast enough to get away, and the farther back down the path he got, the further away the roar sounded. When Morgan finally got to his feet, five-hundred feet down the trail, he looked back to where he had been. The entire pass was blocked by a wall of snow, but there the avalanche had played itself out. The snow slide had quit, leaving a one hundred-foot-deep drift over what had been a cleared path just seconds ago. Somewhere under that one-hundred feet of snow, Morgan knew, lay the bodies of Chapel and the men who were with him.

He chuckled. Synonyms, Bannister had said. Two words meaning the same thing. Like church and chapel, or, put capitol letters to the words and they become Church and Chapel.

Morgan's horse and three of the mules had gotten away from the slide, and Morgan saw them standing quietly, shaking in fear, though not understanding what had just happened. He walked over to his horse and stood there for a moment, calming him.

A couple of travelers, just now approaching the pass, came up then. They looked at the closed pass in bitter disappointment.

"My God, look at that, Charlie," one of them said. "You was right, that was an avalanche. The whole pass is closed."

"Damn!" Charlie said. "All that gold on the other side an' we can't get to it!"

"Maybe there's another way."

"How 'bout you, Mister? You know another way?" one of them asked, hopefully.

"No," Morgan said. He started back down the path.

"Yeah. Well if you don't know any other way, then where are you goin'?" Charlie yelled.

"I'm goin' home," Morgan said.